KAZUO ISHIGURO

A Pale View of Hills

Kazuo Ishiguro is the author of seven other novels, including *Never Let Me Go* and *The Remains of the Day*,
which have been adapted into films. Ishiguro's work
has been translated into forty languages and has won
him many honors, including the Booker Prize, the
Order of the British Empire for service to literature, and
the French decoration Chevalier de l'Ordre des Arts et
des Lettres. In 2017 he was awarded the Nobel Prize in
Literature.

INTERNATIONAL

Books by Kazuo Ishiguro

A Pale View
of Hills

A Pale View of Hills

KAZUO ISHIGURO

VINTAGE INTERNATIONAL
VINTAGE BOOKS
A DIVISION OF PENGUIN RANDOM HOUSE LLC
NEW YORK

First Vintage International Edition, September 1990

Vintage is a registered trademark and Vintage International and colophon are
trademarks of Penguin Random House LLC.

Library of Congress Cataloging-in-Publication Data
Ishiguro, Kazuo 1954–
A pale view of the hills / Kazuo Ishiguro.
p. cm. — (Vintage international)
I. Title. II. Series.
[PR6059.S5P35   1990]
823'.914—dc20   90-50178
CIP

Vintage Books Trade Paperback ISBN: 978-0-679-72267-0
eBook ISBN: 978-0-307-82907-8

AUTHOR PHOTOGRAPH COPYRIGHT © NIGEL PARRY

www.vintagebooks.com

Manufactured in the United States of America
50 49 48 47 46 45 44

PART ONE

Chapter One

Niki, the name we finally gave my younger daughter, is not an abbreviation; it was a compromise I reached with her father. For paradoxically it was he who wanted to give her a Japanese name, and I — perhaps out of some selfish desire not to be reminded of the past — insisted on an English one. He finally agreed to Niki, thinking it had some vague echo of the East about it.

She came to see me earlier this year, in April, when the days were still cold and drizzly. Perhaps she had intended to stay longer, I do not know. But my country house and the quiet that surrounds it made her restless, and before long I could see she was anxious to return to her life in London. She listened impatiently to my classical records, flicked through numerous magazines. The telephone rang for her regularly, and she would stride across the carpet, her thin figure squeezed into her tight clothes, taking care to close the door behind her so I would not overhear her conversation. She left after five days.

She did not mention Keiko until the second day. It was a grey windy morning, and we had moved the armchairs nearer the windows to watch the rain falling on my garden.

"Did you expect me to be there?" she asked. "At the funeral, I mean."

"No, I suppose not. I didn't really think you'd come."

"It did upset me, hearing about her. I almost came."

"I never expected you to come."

"People didn't know what was wrong with me," she said. "I didn't tell anybody. I suppose I was embarrassed. They wouldn't understand really, they wouldn't under-

9

stand how I felt about it. Sisters are supposed to be people you're close to, aren't they. You may not like them much, but you're still close to them. That's just not how it was though. I don't even remember what she looked like now."

"Yes, it's quite a time since you saw her."

"I just remember her as someone who used to make me miserable. That's what I remember about her. But I was sad though, when I heard."

Perhaps it was not just the quiet that drove my daughter back to London. For although we never dwelt long on the subject of Keiko's death, it was never far away, hovering over us whenever we talked.

Keiko, unlike Niki, was pure Japanese, and more than one newspaper was quick to pick up on this fact. The English are fond of their idea that our race has an instinct for suicide, as if further explanations are unnecessary; for that was all they reported, that she was Japanese and that she had hung herself in her room.

That same evening I was standing at the windows, looking out into the darkness, when I heard Niki say behind me; "What are you thinking about now, Mother?" She was sitting across the settee, a paperback book on her knee.

"I was thinking about someone I knew once. A woman I knew once."

"Someone you knew when you . . . before you came to England?"

"I knew her when I was living in Nagasaki, if that's what you mean." She continued to watch me, so I added: "A long time ago. Long before I met your father."

She seemed satisfied and with some vague comment returned to her book. In many ways Niki is an affectionate child. She had not come simply to see how I had taken the news of Keiko's death; she had come to me out of a sense of mission. For in recent years she has taken it upon herself to admire certain aspects of my past, and she had come prepared to tell me things were no different now, that I should have no regrets for those choices I once made. In short, to reassure me I was not responsible for Keiko's death.

I have no great wish to dwell on Keiko now, it brings me little comfort. I only mention her here because those were the circumstances around Niki's visit this April, and because it was during that visit I remembered Sachiko again after all this time. I never knew Sachiko well. In fact our friendship was no more than a matter of some several weeks one summer many years ago.

The worst days were over by then. American soldiers were as numerous as ever — for there was fighting in Korea — but in Nagasaki, after what had gone before, those were days of calm and relief. The world had a feeling of change about it.

My husband and I lived in an area to the east of the city, a short tram journey from the centre of town. A river ran near us, and I was once told that before the war a small village had grown up on the riverbank. But then the bomb had fallen and afterwards all that remained were charred ruins. Rebuilding had got under way and in time four concrete buildings had been erected, each containing forty or so separate apartments. Of the four, our block had been built last and it marked the point where the rebuilding programme had come to a halt; between us and the river lay an expanse of wasteground, several acres of dried mud and ditches. Many complained it was a health hazard, and indeed the drainage was appalling. All year round there were craters filled with stagnant water, and in the summer months the mosquitoes became intolerable. From time to time officials were to be seen pacing out measurements or scribbling down notes, but the months went by and nothing was done.

The occupants of the apartment blocks were much like

11

ourselves — young married couples, the husbands having found good employment with expanding firms. Many of the apartments were owned by the firms, who rented them to employees at a generous rate. Each apartment was identical; the floors were tatami, the bathrooms and kitchens of a Western design. They were small and rather difficult to keep cool during the warmer months, but on the whole the feeling amongst the occupants seemed one of satisfaction. And yet I remember an unmistakable air of transience there, as if we were all of us waiting for the day we could move to something better.

One wooden cottage had survived both the devastation of the war and the government bulldozers. I could see it from our window, standing alone at the end of that expanse of wasteground, practically on the edge of the river. It was the kind of cottage often seen in the countryside, with a tiled roof sloping almost to the ground. Often, during my empty moments, I would stand at my window gazing at it.

To judge from the attention attracted by Sachiko's arrival, I was not alone in gazing at that cottage. There was much talk about two men seen working there one day — as to whether or not they were government workers. Later there was talk that a woman and her little girl were living there, and I saw them myself on several occasions, making their way across the ditchy ground.

It was towards the beginning of summer — I was in my third or fourth month of pregnancy by then — when I first watched that large American car, white and battered, bumping its way over the wasteground towards the river. It was well into the evening, and the sun setting behind the cottage gleamed a moment against the metal.

Then one afternoon I heard two women talking at the tram stop, about the woman who had moved into the derelict house by the river. One was explaining to her companion how she had spoken to the woman that morning and had received a clear snub. Her companion agreed the newcomer seemed unfriendly — proud probably. She must be thirty at the youngest, they thought, for the child was at least ten. The first woman said the stranger had spoken with a Tokyo dialect and certainly was not from Nagasaki. They discussed for a while her "American friend", then the woman spoke again of how unfriendly the stranger had been to her that morning.

Now I do not doubt that amongst those women I lived with then, there were those who had suffered, those with sad and terrible memories. But to watch them each day, busily involved with their husbands and their children, I found this hard to believe — that their lives had ever held the tragedies and nightmares of wartime. It was never my intention to appear unfriendly, but it was probably true that I made no special effort to seem otherwise. For at that point in my life, I was still wishing to be left alone.

It was with interest then that I listened to those women talking of Sachiko. I can recall quite vividly that afternoon at the tram stop. It was one of the first days of bright sunlight after the rainy season in June, and the soaked surfaces of brick and concrete were drying all around us. We were standing on a railway bridge and on one side of the tracks at the foot of the hill could be seen a cluster of roofs, as if houses had come tumbling down the slope. Beyond the houses, a little way off, were our apartment blocks standing like four concrete pillars. I felt a kind of sympathy for Sachiko then, and felt I understood something of that aloofness I had noticed about her when I had watched her from afar.

We were to become friends that summer and for a short time at least I was to be admitted into her confidence. I am not sure now how it was we first met. I remember one afternoon spotting her figure ahead of me on the path leading out of the housing precinct. I was hurrying, but Sachiko walked on with a steady stride. By that point we must have already known each other by name, for I

13

remember calling to her as I got nearer.

Sachiko turned and waited for me to catch up. "Is something wrong?" she asked.

"I'm glad I found you," I said, a little out of breath. "Your daughter, she was fighting just as I came out. Back there near the ditches."

"She was fighting?"

"With two other children. One of them was a boy. It looked a nasty little fight."

"I see." Sachiko began to walk again. I fell in step beside her.

"I don't want to alarm you," I said, "but it did look quite a nasty fight. In fact, I think I saw a cut on your daughter's cheek."

"I see."

"It was back there, on the edge of the wasteground."

"And are they still fighting, do you think?" She continued to walk up the hill.

"Well, no. I saw your daughter running off."

Sachiko looked at me and smiled. "Are you not used to seeing children fight?"

"Well, children do fight, I suppose. But I thought I ought to tell you. And you see, I don't think she's on her way to school. The other children carried on towards the school, but your daughter went back towards the river."

Sachiko made no reply and continued to walk up the hill.

"As a matter of fact," I continued, "I'd meant to mention this to you before. You see, I've seen your daughter on a number of occasions recently. I wonder, perhaps, if she hasn't been playing truant a little."

The path forked at the top of the hill. Sachiko stopped and we turned to each other.

"It's very kind of you to be so concerned, Etsuko," she said. "So very kind. I'm sure you'll make a splendid mother."

I had supposed previously — like the women at the tram

stop — that Sachiko was a woman of thirty or so. But possibly her youthful figure had been deceiving, for she had the face of an older person. She was gazing at me with a slightly amused expression, and something in the way she did so caused me to laugh self-consciously.

"I do appreciate your coming to find me like this," she went on. "But as you see, I'm rather busy just now. I have to go into Nagasaki."

"I see. I just thought it best to come and tell you, that's all."

For a moment, she continued to look at me with her amused expression. Then she said: "How kind you are. Now please excuse me. I must get into town." She bowed, then turned towards the path that led up towards the tram stop.

"It's just that she had a cut on her face," I said, raising my voice a little. "And the river's quite dangerous in places. I thought it best to come and tell you."

She turned and looked at me once more. "If you have nothing else to concern yourself with, Etsuko," she said, "then perhaps you'd care to look after my daughter for the day. I'll be back sometime in the afternoon. I'm sure you'll get on very well with her."

"I wouldn't object, if that's what you wish. I must say, your daughter seems quite young to be left on her own all day."

"How kind you are," Sachiko said again. Then she smiled once more. "Yes, I'm sure you'll make a splendid mother."

After parting with Sachiko, I made my way down the hill and back through the housing precinct. I soon found myself back outside our apartment block, facing that expanse of wasteground. Seeing no sign of the little girl, I was about to go inside, but then caught sight of some movement along the riverbank. Mariko must previously have been crouching down, for now I could see her small figure quite clearly across the muddy ground. At first, I felt the urge to forget the whole matter and return to my housework. Eventually, however, I began making my way towards her, taking care to avoid the ditches.

As far as I remember, that was the first occasion I spoke to Mariko. Quite probably there was nothing so unusual about her behaviour that morning, for, after all, I was a stranger to the child and she had every right to regard me with suspicion. And if in fact I did experience a curious feeling of unease at the time, it was probably nothing more than a simple response to Mariko's manner.

The river that morning was still quite high and flowing swiftly after the rainy season a few weeks earlier. The ground sloped down steeply before it reached the water's edge, and the mud at the foot of the slope, where the little girl was standing, looked distinctly wetter. Mariko was dressed in a simple cotton dress which ended at her knees, and her short trimmed hair made her face look boyish. She looked up, not smiling, to where I stood at the top of the muddy slope.

"Hello," I said, "I was just speaking with your mother. You must be Mariko-San."

The little girl continued to stare up at me, saying nothing. What I had thought earlier to be a wound on her cheek, I now saw to be a smudge of mud.

"Shouldn't you be at school?" I asked.

She remained silent for a moment. Then she said: "I don't go to school."

"But all children must go to school. Don't you like to go?"

"I don't go to school."

"But hasn't your mother sent you to a school here?"

Mariko did not reply. Instead, she took a step away from me.

"Careful," I said. "You'll fall into the water. It's very slippery."

She continued to stare up at me from the bottom of the

16

slope. I could see her small shoes lying in the mud beside her. Her bare feet, like her shoes, were covered in mud.

"I was just speaking with your mother," I said, smiling at her reassuringly. "She said it would be perfectly all right if you came and waited for her at my house. It's just over there, that building there. You could come and try some cakes I made yesterday. Would you like that, Mariko-San? And you could tell me all about yourself."

Mariko continued to watch me carefully. Then, without taking her eyes off me, she crouched down and picked up her shoes. At first, I took this as a sign that she was about to follow me. But then as she continued to stare up at me, I realized she was holding her shoes in readiness to run away.

"I'm not going to hurt you," I said, with a nervous laugh. "I'm a friend of your mother's."

As far as I remember, that was all that took place between us that morning. I had no wish to alarm the child further, and before long I turned and made my way back across the wasteground. The child's response had, it is true, upset me somewhat; for in those days, such small things were capable of arousing in me every kind of misgiving about motherhood. I told myself the episode was insignificant, and that in any case, further opportunities to make friends with the little girl were bound to present themselves over the coming days. As it was, I did not speak to Mariko again until one afternoon a fortnight or so later.

I had never been inside the cottage prior to that afternoon, and I had been rather surprised when Sachiko had asked me in. In fact, I had sensed immediately that she had done so with something in mind, and as it turned out, I was not mistaken.

The cottage was tidy, but I remember a kind of stark shabbiness about the place; the wooden beams that crossed

17

the ceiling looked old and insecure, and a faint odour of dampness lingered everywhere. At the front of the cottage, the main partitions had been left wide open to allow the sunlight in across the veranda. For all that, much of the place remained in shadow.

Mariko was lying in the corner furthest from the sunlight. I could see something moving beside her in the shade, and when I came closer, saw a large cat curled up on the tatami.

"Hello, Mariko-San," I said. "Don't you remember me?"

She stopped stroking the cat and looked up.

"We met the other day," I went on. "Don't you remember? You were by the river."

The little girl showed no signs of recognition. She looked at me for a while, then began to stroke her cat again. Behind me, I could hear Sachiko preparing the tea on the open stove at the centre of the room. I was about to go over to her, when Mariko said suddenly: "She's going to have kittens."

"Oh really? How nice."

"Do you want a kitten?"

"That's very kind of you, Mariko-San. We'll see. But I'm sure they'll all find nice homes."

"Why don't you take a kitten?" the child said. "The other woman said she'd take one."

"We'll see, Mariko-San. Which other lady was this?"

"The other woman. The woman from across the river. She said she'd take one."

"But I don't think anyone lives over there, Mariko-San. It's just trees and forest over there."

"She said she'd take me to her house. She lives across the river. I didn't go with her."

I looked at the child for a second. Then a thought struck me and I laughed.

"But that was me, Mariko-San. Don't you remember? I asked you to come to my house while your mother was away in the town."

18

Mariko looked up at me again. "Not you," she said. "The other woman. The woman from across the river. She was here last night. While Mother was away."

"Last night? While your mother was away?"

"She said she'd take me to her house, but I didn't go with her. Because it was dark. She said we could take the lantern with us" — she gestured towards a lantern hung on the wall — "but I didn't go with her. Because it was dark."

Behind me, Sachiko had got to her feet and was looking at her daughter. Mariko became silent, then turned away and began once more to stroke her cat.

"Let's go out on the veranda,' Sachiko said to me. She was holding the tea things on a tray. "It's cooler out there."

We did as she suggested, leaving Mariko in her corner. From the veranda, the river itself was hidden from view, but I could see where the ground sloped down and the mud became wetter as it approached the water. Sachiko seated herself on a cushion and began to pour the tea.

"The place is alive with stray cats," she said. "I'm not so optimistic about these kittens."

"Yes, there are so many strays," I said. "It's such a shame. Did Mariko find her cat around here somewhere?"

"No, we brought that creature with us. I'd have preferred to leave it behind myself, but Mariko wouldn't hear of it."

"You brought it all the way from Tokyo?"

"Oh no. We've been living in Nagasaki for almost a year now. On the other side of the city."

"Oh really? I didn't realize that. You lived there with . . . with friends?"

Sachiko stopped pouring and looked at me, the teapot held in both hands. I saw in her gaze something of that amused expression with which she had observed me on that earlier occasion.

"I'm afraid you're quite wrong, Etsuko," she said, eventually. Then she began to pour the tea again. "We were staying at my uncle's house."

19

"I assure you, I was merely . . ."

"Yes, of course. So there's no need to get embarrassed, is there?" She laughed and passed me my teacup. "I'm sorry, Etsuko, I don't mean to tease you. As a matter of fact, I did have something to ask you. A little favour." Sachiko began to pour tea into her own cup, and as she did so, a more serious air seemed to enter her manner. Then she put down the teapot and looked at me. "You see, Etsuko, certain arrangements I made have not gone as planned. As a result, I find myself in need of money. Not a great deal, you understand. Just a small amount."

"I quite understand," I said, lowering my voice. "It must be very difficult for you, with Mariko-San to think of."

"Etsuko, may I ask a favour of you?"

I bowed. "I have some savings of my own," I said, almost in a whisper. "I'd be pleased to be of some assistance."

To my surprise, Sachiko laughed loudly. "You're very kind," she said. "But I didn't in fact want you to lend me money. I had something else in mind. You mentioned something the other day. A friend of yours who ran a noodle shop."

"Mrs Fujiwara, you mean?"

"You were saying she may want an assistant. A small job like that would be very useful to me."

"Well," I said, uncertainly, "I could enquire if you wish."

"That would be very kind." Sachiko looked at me for a moment. "But you look rather unsure about it, Etsuko."

"Not at all. I'll enquire when I next see her. But I was just wondering" — I lowered my voice again — "who would look after your daughter during the day?"

"Mariko? She could help at the noodle shop. She's quite capable of being useful."

"I'm sure she is. But you see, I'm not certain how Mrs Fujiwara would feel. After all, Mariko should in reality be at school during the day."

"I assure you, Etsuko, Mariko won't be the slightest

20

problem. Besides, the schools are closing next week. And I'll make sure she won't get in the way. You can rest assured on that."

I bowed again. "I'll enquire when I next see her."

"I'm very grateful to you." Sachiko took a sip from her teacup. "In fact, perhaps I could ask you to see your friend within the next few days."

"I'll try."

"You're so kind."

We fell silent for a moment. My attention had been caught earlier by Sachiko's teapot; it appeared a fine piece of craftsmanship made from a pale china. The teacup I now held in my hand was of the same delicate material. As we sat drinking our tea, I was struck, not for the first time, by the odd contrast of the tea-set alongside the shabbiness of the cottage and the muddy ground beneath the veranda. When I looked up, I realized Sachiko had been watching me.

"I'm used to good crockery, Etsuko," she said. "You see, I don't always live like" — she waved a hand towards the cottage — "like this. Of course, I don't mind a little discomfort. But about some things, I'm still rather discerning."

I bowed, saying nothing. Sachiko, also, began to study her teacup. She continued to examine it, turning it carefully in her hands. Then suddenly she said: "I suppose it's true to say I stole this tea-set. Still, I don't suppose my uncle will miss it much."

I looked at her, somewhat surprised. Sachiko put the teacup down in front of her and waved away some flies.

"You were living at your uncle's house, you say?" I asked.

She nodded slowly. "A most beautiful house. With a pond in the garden. Very different from these present surroundings."

For a moment, we both glanced towards the inside of the

21

cottage. Mariko was lying in her corner, just as we had left her, her back turned towards us. She appeared to be talking quietly to her cat.

"I didn't realize", I said, when neither of us had spoken for some time, "that anyone lived across the river."

Sachiko turned and glanced towards the trees on the far bank. "No, I haven't seen anyone there."

"But your babysitter. Mariko was saying she came from over there."

"I have no babysitter, Etsuko. I know nobody here."

"Mariko was telling me about some lady . . ."

"Please don't pay any attention."

"You mean she was just making it up?"

For a brief moment, Sachiko seemed to be considering something. Then she said: "Yes. She was just making it up."

"Well, I suppose children often do things like that."

Sachiko nodded. "When you become a mother, Etsuko," she said, smiling, "you'll need to get used to such things."

We drifted on to other subjects then. Those were early days in our friendship and we talked mainly of little things. It was not until one morning some weeks later that I heard Mariko mention again a woman who had approached her.

Chapter Two

In those days, returning to the Nakagawa district still provoked in me mixed emotions of sadness and pleasure. It is a hilly area, and climbing again those steep narrow streets between the clusters of houses never failed to fill me with a deep sense of loss. Though not a place I visited on casual impulse, I was unable to stay away for long.

Calling on Mrs Fujiwara aroused in me much the same mixture of feelings; for she had been amongst my mother's closest friends, a kindly woman with hair that was by then turning grey. Her noodle shop was situated in a busy sidestreet; it had a concrete forecourt under the cover of an extended roof and it was there her customers ate, at the wooden tables and benches. She did a lot of trade with office workers during their lunch breaks and again on their way home, but at other times of the day the clientele became sparse.

I was a little anxious that afternoon, for it was the first time I had called at the shop since Sachiko had started to work there. I felt concerned — on both their behalves — especially since I was not sure how genuinely Mrs Fujiwara had wanted an assistant. It was a hot day, and the little sidestreet was alive with people. I was glad to come into the shade.

Mrs Fujiwara was pleased to see me. She sat me down at a table, then went to fetch some tea. Customers were few that afternoon — perhaps there were none, I do not remember — and Sachiko was not to be seen. When Mrs Fujiwara came back, I asked her: "How is my friend getting along? Is she managing all right?"

23

"Your friend?" Mrs Fujiwara looked over her shoulder towards the doorway of the kitchen. "She was peeling prawns. I expect she'll be out soon." Then, as if on second thoughts, she got to her feet and walked a little way towards the doorway. "Sachiko-San," she called. "Etsuko is here." I heard a voice reply from within.

As she sat down again, Mrs Fujiwara reached over and touched my stomach. "It's beginning to show now," she said. "You must take good care from now on."

"I don't do a great deal anyway," I said. "I lead a very easy life."

"That's good. I remember my first time, there was an earthquake, quite a large one. I was carrying Kazuo then. He came perfectly healthy though. Try not to worry too much, Etsuko."

"I try not to." I glanced towards the kitchen door. "Is my friend getting on well here?"

Mrs Fujiwara followed my gaze towards the kitchen. Then she turned to me again and said: "I expect so. You're good friends, are you?"

"Yes. I haven't found many friends where we live. I'm very glad to have met Sachiko."

"Yes. That was fortunate." She sat there looking at me for several seconds. "Etsuko, you're looking rather tired today."

"I suppose I am." I laughed a little. "It's only to be expected, I suppose."

"Yes, of course." Mrs Fujiwara kept looking into my face. "But I meant you looked a little — miserable."

"Miserable? I certainly don't feel it. I'm just a little tired, but otherwise I've never been happier."

"That's good. You must keep your mind on happy things now. Your child. And the future."

"Yes, I will. Thinking about the child cheers me up."

"Good." She nodded, still keeping her gaze on me. "Your attitude makes all the difference. A mother can take

24

all the physical care she likes, she needs a positive attitude to bring up a child."

"Well, I'm certainly looking forward to it," I said, with a laugh. A noise made me look towards the kitchen again, but Sachiko was still not in sight.

"There's a young woman I see every week," Mrs Fujiwara went on. "She must be six or seven months pregnant now. I see her every time I go to visit the cemetery. I've never spoken to her, but she looks so sad, standing there with her husband. It's a shame, a pregnant girl and her husband spending their Sundays thinking about the dead. I know they're being respectful, but all the same, I think it's a shame. They should be thinking about the future."

"I suppose she finds it hard to forget."

"I suppose so. I feel sorry for her. But they should be thinking ahead now. That's no way to bring a child into the world, visiting the cemetery every week."

"Perhaps not."

"Cemeteries are no places for young people. Kazuo comes with me sometimes, but I never insist. It's time he started looking ahead too."

"How is Kazuo?" I asked. "Is his work coming on well?"

"His work's fine. He's expecting to be promoted next month. But he needs to give other things a little thought. He won't be young for ever."

Just then my eye was caught by a small figure standing out in the sunlight amidst the rush of passers-by.

"Why, isn't that Mariko?" I said.

Mrs Fujiwara turned in her seat. "Mariko-San," she called. "Where have you been?"

For a moment, Mariko remained standing out in the street. Then she stepped into the shade of the forecourt, came walking past us and sat down at an empty table nearby.

Mrs Fujiwara watched the little girl, then gave me an uneasy look. She seemed about to say something, but then

25

got to her feet and went over to the little girl.

"Mariko-San, where have you been?" Mrs Fujiwara had lowered her voice, but I was still able to hear. "You're not to keep running off like that. Your mother's very angry with you."

Mariko was studying her fingers. She did not look up at Mrs Fujiwara.

"And Mariko-San, please, you're never to talk to customers like that. Don't you know it's very rude? Your mother's very angry with you."

Mariko went on studying her hands. Behind her, Sachiko appeared in the doorway of the kitchen. Seeing Sachiko that morning, I recall I was struck afresh by the impression that she was indeed older than I had first supposed; with her long hair hidden away inside a handkerchief, the tired areas of skin around her eyes and mouth seemed somehow more pronounced.

"Here's your mother now," said Mrs Fujiwara. "I expect she's very angry with you."

The little girl had remained seated with her back to her mother. Sachiko threw a quick glance towards her, then turned to me with a smile.

"How do you do, Etsuko," she said, with an elegant bow. "What a pleasant surprise to see you here."

At the other end of the forecourt, two women in office clothes were seating themselves at a table. Mrs Fujiwara gestured towards them, then turned to Mariko once more.

"Why don't you go into the kitchen for a little while," she said, in a low voice. "Your mother will show you what to do. It's very easy. I'm sure a clever girl like you could manage."

Mariko gave no sign of having heard. Mrs Fujiwara glanced up at Sachiko, and for a brief instant I thought they exchanged cold glances. Then Mrs Fujiwara turned and went off towards her customers. She appeared to know them, for as she walked across the forecourt, she gave them a familiar greeting.

Sachiko came and sat at the edge of my table. "It's so hot inside that kitchen," she said.

"How are you getting on here?" I asked her.

"How am I getting on? Well, Etsuko, it's certainly an amusing sort of experience, working in a noodle shop. I must say, I never imagined I'd one day find myself scrubbing tables in a place like this. Still" — she laughed quickly — "it's quite amusing."

"I see. And Mariko, is she settling in?"

We both glanced over to Mariko's table; the child was still looking down at her hands.

"Oh, Mariko's fine," said Sachiko. "Of course, she's rather restless at times. But then you'd hardly expect otherwise under the circumstances. It's regrettable, Etsuko, but you see, my daughter doesn't seem to share my sense of humour. She doesn't find it quite so amusing here." Sachiko smiled and glanced towards Mariko again. Then she got to her feet and went over to her.

She asked quietly: "Is it true what Mrs Fujiwara told me?"

The little girl remained silent.

"She says you were being rude to customers again. Is that true?"

Mariko still gave no response.

"Is it true what she told me? Mariko, please answer when you're spoken to."

"The woman came round again," said Mariko. "Last night. While you were gone."

Sachiko looked at her daughter for a second or two. Then she said: "I think you should go inside now. Go on, I'll show you what you have to do."

"She came again last night. She said she'd take me to her house."

"Go on, Mariko, go on into the kitchen and wait for me there."

27

"She's going to show me where she lives."

"Mariko, go inside."

Across the forecourt, Mrs Fujiwara and the two women were laughing loudly about something. Mariko continued to stare at her palms. Sachiko turned away and came back to my table.

'Excuse me a moment, Etsuko," she said. "But I left something boiling. I'll be back in just a moment." Then lowering her voice, she added: "You can hardly expect her to get enthusiastic about a place like this, can you?" She smiled and went towards the kitchen. At the doorway, she turned once more to her daughter.

"Come on, Mariko, come inside."

Mariko did not move. Sachiko shrugged, then disappeared inside the kitchen.

Around that same time, in early summer, Ogata-San came to visit us, his first visit since moving away from Nagasaki earlier that year. He was my husband's father, and it seems rather odd I always thought of him as "Ogata-San", even in those days when that was my own name. But then I had known him as "Ogata-San" for such a long time — since long before I had ever met Jiro — I had never got used to calling him "Father".

There was little family resemblance between Ogata-San and my husband. When I recall Jiro today, I picture a small stocky man wearing a stern expression; my husband was always fastidious about his appearance, and even at home would frequently dress in shirt and tie. I see him now as I saw him so often, seated on the tatami in our living room, hunched forward over his breakfast or supper. I remember he had this same tendency to hunch forward — in a manner not unlike that of a boxer — whether standing or walking. By contrast, his father would always sit with his shoulders flung well back, and had a relaxed, generous manner about

28

him. When he came to visit us that summer, Ogata-San was still in the best of health, displaying a well-built physique and the robust energy of a much younger man.

I remember the morning he first mentioned Shigeo Matsuda. He had been with us for a few days by then, apparently finding the small square room comfortable enough for an extended stay. It was a bright morning and the three of us were finishing breakfast before Jiro left for the office.

"This school reunion of yours," he said to Jiro. "That's tonight, is it?"

"No, tomorrow evening."

"Will you be seeing Shigeo Matsuda?"

"Shigeo? No, I doubt it. He doesn't usually attend these occasions. I'm sorry to be going off and leaving you, Father. I'd rather give the thing a miss, but that may cause offence."

"Don't worry. Etsuko-San will look after me well enough. And these occasions are important."

"I'd take some days off work," Jiro said, "but we're so busy just now. As I say, this order came into the office the day you arrived. A real nuisance."

"Not at all," said his father. "I understand perfectly. It wasn't so long ago I was rushed off my feet with work myself. I'm not so old, you know."

"No, of course."

We ate on in silence for several moments. Then Ogata-San said:

"So you don't think you'll be running into Shigeo Matsuda. But you still see him from time to time?"

"Not so often these days. We've gone such separate ways since we got older."

"Yes, this is what happens. Pupils all go separate ways, and then they find it so difficult to keep in touch. That's why these reunions are so important. One shouldn't be so quick to forget old allegiances. And it's good to take a glance back now and then, it helps keep things in perspective. Yes, I think you should certainly go along tomorrow."

"Perhaps Father will still be with us on Sunday," my husband said. "Then perhaps we could go out somewhere for the day."

"Yes, we can do that. A splendid idea. But if you have work to do, it doesn't matter in the least."

"No, I think I can leave Sunday free. I'm sorry to be so busy at the moment."

"Have you asked any of your old teachers along tomorrow?" Ogata-San asked.

"Not that I know of."

"It's a shame teachers aren't asked more often to these occasions. I was asked along from time to time. And when I was younger, we always made a point of inviting our teachers. I think it's only proper. It's an opportunity for a teacher to see the fruits of his work, and for the pupils to express their gratitude to him. I think it's only proper that teachers are present."

"Yes, perhaps you have a point."

"Men these days forget so easily to whom they owe their education."

"Yes, you're very right."

My husband finished eating and laid down his chopsticks. I poured him some tea.

"An odd little thing happened the other day," Ogata-San said. "In retrospect, I suppose it's rather amusing. I was at the library in Nagasaki, and I came across this periodical — a teachers' periodical. I'd never heard of it, it wasn't in existence in my days. To read it, you'd think all the teachers in Japan were communists now."

"Apparently communism is growing in the country," my husband said.

"Your friend Shigeo Matsuda had written in it. Now imagine my surprise when I saw my name mentioned in his article. I didn't think I was so noteworthy these days."

"I'm sure Father is still remembered very well in Nagasaki," I put in.

"It was quite extraordinary. He was talking about Dr Endo and myself, about our retirements. If I understood him correctly, he was implying that the profession was well rid of us. In fact, he went so far as to suggest we should have been dismissed at the end of the war. Quite extraordinary."

"Are you sure it's the same Shigeo Matsuda?" asked Jiro.

"The same one. From Kuriyama Highschool. Extraordinary. I remember when he used to come to our house, to play with you. Your mother used to spoil him. I asked the librarian if I could buy a copy, and she said she would order one for me. I'll show it to you."

"It seems very disloyal," I said.

"I was so surprised," Ogata-San said, turning to me. "And I was the one who introduced him to the headmaster at Kuriyama."

Jiro drank up his tea and wiped his mouth with his napkin. "It's very regrettable. As I say, I haven't seen Shigeo for some time. I'm sorry, Father, but you must excuse me now or I'll be late."

"Why certainly. Have a good day at work."

Jiro stepped down to the entryway, where he started to put on his shoes. I said to Ogata-San: "Someone who reached your position, Father, must expect a little criticism. That's only natural."

"Of course," he said, breaking out into a laugh. "No, don't concern yourself about it, Etsuko. I hadn't given it a second thought. I just happened to think of it because Jiro was going to his reunion. I wonder if Endo read the article."

"I hope you have a good day, Father," Jiro called from the entryway. "I'll try to be back a little early if I can."

"Nonsense, don't make such a fuss. Your work is important."

A little later that morning, Ogata-San emerged from his room dressed in his jacket and tie.

"Are you going out, Father?" I asked.

"I thought I'd just pay a visit to Dr Endo."

"Dr Endo?"

"Yes, I thought I'd go and see how he was keeping these days."

"But you're not going before lunch, are you?"

"I thought I'd better go quite soon," he said, looking at his watch. "Endo lives a little way outside Nagasaki now. I'll need to get a train."

"Well, let me pack you a lunch-box, it won't take a minute."

"Why, thank you, Etsuko. In that case I'll wait a few minutes. In fact, I was hoping you'd offer to pack me lunch."

"Then you should have asked," I said, getting to my feet. "You won't always get what you want just by hinting like that, Father."

"But I knew you'd pick me up correctly, Etsuko. I have faith in you."

I went through to the kitchen, put on some sandals and stepped down to the tiled floor. A few minutes later, the partition slid open and Ogata-San appeared at the doorway. He seated himself at the threshold to watch me working.

"What is that you're cooking me there?"

"Nothing much. Just left-overs from last night. At such short notice, you don't deserve any better."

"And yet you'll manage to turn it into something quite appetizing, I'm sure. What's that you're doing with the egg? That's not a left-over too, is it?"

"I'm adding an omelette. You're very fortunate, Father, I'm in such a generous mood."

32

"An omelette. You must teach me how to do that. Is it difficult?"

"Extremely difficult. It would be hopeless you trying to learn at this stage."

"But I'm very keen to learn. And what do you mean 'at this stage'? I'm still young enough to learn many new things."

"Are you really planning on becoming a cook, Father?"

"It's nothing to laugh at. I've come to appreciate cooking over the years. It's an art, I'm convinced of it, just as noble as painting or poetry. It's not appreciated simply because the product disappears so quickly."

"Persevere with painting, Father. You do it much better."

"Painting." He gave a sigh. "It doesn't give me the satisfaction it once did. No, I think I should learn to cook omelettes as well as you do, Etsuko. You must show me before I go back to Fukuoka."

"You wouldn't think it such an art once you'd learnt how it was done. Perhaps women should keep these things secret."

He laughed, as if to himself, then continued to watch me quietly.

"Which are you hoping for, Etsuko?" he asked, eventually. "A boy or a girl?"

"I really don't mind. If it's a boy we could name him after you."

"Really? Is that a promise?"

"On second thoughts I don't know. I was forgetting what Father's first name was. Seiji — that's an ugly sort of name."

"But that's only because you find me ugly, Etsuko. I remember one class of pupils decided I resembled a hippopotamus. But you shouldn't be put off by such outer trappings."

"That's true. Well, we'll have to see what Jiro thinks."

"Yes."

"But I'd like my son to be named after you, Father "

"That would make me very happy." He smiled and gave me a small bow. "But then I know how irritating it is when relatives insist on having children named after them. I remember the time my wife and I argued over what to call Jiro. I wanted to name him after an uncle of mine, but my wife disliked this practice of naming children after relatives. Of course, she had her way in the end. Keiko was a hard woman to budge."

"Keiko is a nice name. Perhaps if it's a girl we could call her Keiko."

"You shouldn't make such promises so rashly. You'll make an old man very disappointed if you don't keep to them."

"I'm sorry, I was just thinking aloud."

"And besides, Etsuko, I'm sure there are others you'd prefer to name your child after. Others you were closer to."

"Perhaps. But if it's a boy I'd like him to be named after you. You were like a father to me once."

"Am I no longer like a father to you?"

"Yes, of course. But it's different."

"Jiro is a good husband to you, I hope."

"Of course. I couldn't be happier."

"And the child will make you happy."

"Yes. It couldn't have happened at a better time. We're quite settled here now, and Jiro's work is going well. This is the ideal time for this to have happened."

"So you're happy?"

"Yes, I'm very happy."

"Good. I'm happy for you both."

"There, it's all ready for you." I handed him the lacquer lunch-box.

"Ah yes, the left-overs," he said, receiving it with a dramatic bow. He lifted the lid a little. "It looks delightful though."

34

When I eventually went back into the living room, Ogata-San was putting on his shoes in the entryway.

"Tell me, Etsuko," he said, not looking up from his laces. "Have you met this Shigeo Matsuda?"

"Once or twice. He used to visit us after we were married."

"But he and Jiro aren't such close friends these days?"

"Hardly. We exchange greeting cards, but that's all."

"I'm going to suggest to Jiro he writes to his friend. Shigeo should apologize. Or else I'll have to insist Jiro disassociates himself from that young man."

"I see."

"I thought of suggesting it to him earlier, when we were talking at breakfast. But then that kind of talk is best left till the evening."

"You're probably right."

Ogata-San thanked me once more for the lunch-box before leaving.

As it turned out, he did not bring the matter up that night. They both seemed tired when they came in and spent most of the evening reading newspapers, speaking little. And only once did Ogata-San mention Dr Endo. That was at supper, and he said simply: "Endo seemed well. He misses his work though. After all, the man lived for it."

In bed that night, before we fell asleep, I said to Jiro: "I hope Father's quite content with the way we're receiving him."

"What else can he expect?" my husband said. "Why don't you take him out somewhere if you're so worried."

"Will you be working on Saturday afternoon?"

"How can I afford not to? I'm behind schedule as it is. He happened to choose the most difficult of times to visit me. It's just too bad."

"But we could still go out on Sunday, couldn't we?"

35

I have a feeling I did not receive a reply then, though I lay gazing up into the darkness waiting. Jiro was often tired after a day's work and not in the mood for conversation.

In any case, it seems I was worrying unduly about Ogata-San, for his visit that summer turned out to be one of his lengthiest. I remember he was still with us that night Sachiko knocked on our apartment door.

She was wearing a dress I had never seen before, and there was a shawl wrapped around her shoulders. Her face had been carefully made up, but a thin strand of hair had come loose and was hanging over her cheek.

"I'm sorry to disturb you, Etsuko," she said, smiling. "I was wondering if by any chance Mariko was here."

"Mariko? Why, no."

"Well, never mind. You haven't seen her at all?"

"I'm afraid not. You've lost her?"

"There's no need to look like that," she said, with a laugh. "It's just that she wasn't in the cottage when I got back, that's all. I'm sure I'll find her very soon."

We were talking at the entryway, and I became aware of Jiro and Ogata-San looking towards us. I introduced Sachiko, and they all bowed to each other.

"This is worrying," Ogata-San said. "Perhaps we'd better phone the police straight away."

"There's no need for that," said Sachiko. "I'm sure I'll find her."

"But perhaps it's best to be safe and phone anyway."

"No really" — a slight hint of irritation had entered Sachiko's voice — "there's no need. I'm sure I'll find her."

"I'll help you look for her," I said, starting to put on my jacket.

My husband looked at me disapprovingly. He seemed about to speak, but then stopped himself. In the end, he said: "It's almost dark now."

"Really, Etsuko, there's no need to make such a fuss," Sachiko was saying. "But if you don't mind coming out for a minute, I'll be most grateful."

"Take care, Etsuko," Ogata-San said. "And phone the police if you don't find the child soon."

We descended the flight of stairs. Outside it was still warm, and across the wasteground the sun had sunk very low, highlighting the muddy furrows.

"Have you looked around the housing precinct?" I asked.

"No, not yet."

"Let's look then." I began to walk rapidly. "Does Mariko have friends she may be with?"

"I don't think so. Really, Etsuko" — Sachiko laughed and put a hand on my arm — "there's no need to be so alarmed. Nothing will have happened to her. In fact, Etsuko, I really came round because I wanted to tell you some news. You see, it's all been settled at last. We're leaving for America within the next few days."

"America?" Perhaps because of Sachiko's hand on my arm, perhaps out of sheer surprise, I stopped walking.

"Yes, America. You've no doubt heard of such a place." She seemed pleased at my astonishment.

I began to walk again. Our precinct was an expanse of paved concrete, interrupted occasionally by thin young trees planted when the buildings had gone up. Above us, lights had come on in most of the windows.

"Aren't you going to ask me anything more?" Sachiko said, catching up with me. "Aren't you going to ask me why I'm going? And who I'm going with?"

"I'm very glad if this is what you wanted," I said. "But perhaps we should find your daughter first."

"Etsuko, you must understand, there's nothing I'm ashamed of. There's nothing I want to hide from anyone. Please ask me anything you want, I'm not ashamed."

"I thought perhaps we should find your daughter first.

We can talk later."

"Very well, Etsuko," she said, with a laugh. "Let's find Mariko first."

We searched the playing areas and walked around each of the apartment blocks. Soon we found ourselves back where we had started. Then I spotted two women talking by the main entrance to one of the apartment blocks.

"Perhaps those ladies over there could help us," I said.

Sachiko did not move. She looked over towards the two women, then said: "I doubt it."

"But they may have seen her. They may have seen your daughter."

Sachiko continued to look at the women. Then she gave a short laugh and shrugged. "Very well," she said. "Let's give them something to gossip about. It's no concern of mine."

We walked over to them and Sachiko politely and calmly made her enquiries. The women exchanged concerned looks, but neither had seen the little girl. Sachiko assured them there was no cause for alarm, and we took our leave.

"I'm sure that made their day," she said to me. "Now they'll have something to talk about."

"I'm sure they had no malicious thoughts whatsoever. They both seemed genuinely concerned."

"You're so kind, Etsuko, but there's really no need to convince me of such things. You see, it's never been any concern to me what people like that thought, and I care even less now."

We stopped walking. I threw a glance around me, and up at the apartment windows. "Where else could she be?" I said.

"You see, Etsuko, there's nothing I'm ashamed of. There's nothing I want to hide from you. Or from those women, for that matter."

"Do you think we should search by the river?"

"The river? Oh, I've looked along there."

"What about the other side? Perhaps she's over on the other side."

"I doubt it, Etsuko. In fact, if I know my daughter, she'll be back at the cottage at this very moment. Probably rather pleased with herself to have caused this fuss."

"Well, let's go and see."

When we came back to the edge of the wasteground, the sun was disappearing behind the river, silhouetting the willow trees along the bank.

"There's no need for you to come with me," Sachiko said. "I'll find her in good time."

"It's all right. I'll come with you."

"Very well then. Come with me."

We began walking towards the cottage. I was wearing sandals and found it hard going on the uneven earth.

"How long were you out?" I asked. Sachiko was a pace or two ahead of me; she did not reply at first, and I thought possibly she had not heard me. "How long were you out?" I repeated.

"Oh, not long."

"How long? Half an hour? Longer?"

"About three or four hours, I suppose."

"I see."

We continued our way across the muddy ground, doing our best to avoid any puddles. As we approached the cottage, I said: "Perhaps we should look over on the other side, just in case."

"The woods? My daughter wouldn't be over there. Let's go and look in the cottage. There's no need to look so worried, Etsuko." She laughed again, but I thought her voice wobbled a little as she did so.

The cottage, having no electricity, was in darkness. I waited in the entryway while Sachiko stepped up to the tatami. She called her daughter's name and slid back the partitions to the two smaller rooms that adjoined the main one. I stood listening to her moving around in the darkness, then she came back to the entryway.

"Perhaps you're right," she said. "We'd better look on the other bank."

Along the river the air was full of insects. We walked in silence, towards the small wooden bridge further downstream. Beyond it, on the opposite bank, were the woods Sachiko had mentioned earlier.

We were crossing the bridge, when Sachiko turned to me and said rapidly: "We went to a bar in the end. We were going to go to the cinema, to a film with Gary Cooper, but there was a long queue. The town was very crowded and a lot of people were drunk. We went to a bar in the end and they gave us a little room to ourselves."

"I see."

"I suppose you don't go to bars, do you, Etsuko?"

"No, I don't."

That was the first time I had crossed to the far side of the river. The ground felt soft, almost marshy under my feet. Perhaps it is just my fancy that I felt a cold touch of unease there on that bank, a feeling not unlike premonition, which caused me to walk with renewed urgency towards the darkness of the trees before us.

Sachiko stopped me, grasping my arm. Following her gaze, I could see a short way along the bank something like a bundle lying on the grass, close to the river's edge. It was just discernible in the gloom, a few shades darker than the ground around it. My first impulse was to run towards it, but then I realized Sachiko was standing quite still, gazing towards the object.

"What is it?" I said, rather stupidly.

"It's Mariko," she said, quietly. And when she turned to me there was a strange look in her eyes.

Chapter Three

It is possible that my memory of these events will have grown hazy with time, that things did not happen in quite the way they come back to me today. But I remember with some distinctness that eerie spell which seemed to bind the two of us as we stood there in the coming darkness looking towards that shape further down the bank. Then the spell broke and we both began to run. As we came nearer, I saw Mariko lying curled on her side, knees hunched, her back towards us. Sachiko reached the spot a little ahead of me, I being slowed by my pregnancy, and she was standing over the child when I joined her. Mariko's eyes were open and at first I thought she was dead. But then I saw them move and they stared up at us with a peculiar blankness.

Sachiko dropped on to one knee and lifted the child's head. Mariko continued to stare.

"Mariko-San, are you all right?" I said, a little out of breath.

She did not reply. Sachiko too was silent, examining her daughter, turning her in her arms as if she were a fragile, but senseless doll. I noticed the blood on Sachiko's sleeve, then saw it was coming from Mariko.

"We'd better call someone," I said.

"It's not serious," Sachiko said. "It's just a graze. See, it's just a small cut."

Mariko had been lying in a puddle and one side of her short dress was soaked in dark water. The blood was coming from a wound on the inside of her thigh.

"What happened?" Sachiko said to her daughter. "What happened to you?"

Mariko went on looking at her mother.

"She's probably shocked," I said. "Perhaps it's best not to question her immediately."

Sachiko brought Mariko to her feet.

"We were very worried about you, Mariko-San," I said. The little girl gave me a suspicious look, then turned away and started to walk. She walked quite steadily; the wound on her leg did not seem to trouble her unduly.

We walked back over the bridge and along the river. The two of them walked in front of me, not talking. It was completely dark by the time we reached the cottage.

Sachiko took Mariko into the bathroom. I lit the stove in the centre of the main room to make some tea. Aside from the stove, an old hanging lantern Sachiko had lit provided the only source of light, and large areas of the room remained in shadow. In one corner several tiny black kittens aroused by our arrival started to move restlessly. Their claws, catching in the tatami, made a scuttling noise.

When they appeared again, both mother and daughter had changed into kimonos. They went through to one of the small adjoining rooms and I continued to wait for some time. The sound of Sachiko's voice came through the screen.

Finally, Sachiko came out alone. "It's still very hot," she remarked. She crossed the room and slid apart the partitions which opened out on to the veranda.

"How is she?" I asked.

"She's all right. The cut's nothing." Sachiko sat down in the breeze, next to the partitions.

"Shall we report the matter to the police?"

"The police? But what is there to report? Mariko says she was climbing a tree and fell. That's how she got her cut."

"So she wasn't with anyone tonight?"

"No. Who could she have been with?"

"And what about this woman?" I said.

"What woman?"

42

"This woman Mariko talks about. Are you still certain she's imaginary?"

Sachiko sighed. "She's not entirely imaginary, I suppose," she said. "She's just someone Mariko saw once. Once, when she was much younger."

"But do you think she could have been here tonight, this woman?"

Sachiko gave a laugh. "No, Etsuko, that's quite impossible. In any case, that woman's dead. Believe me, Etsuko, all this about a woman, it's just a little game Mariko likes to play when she means to be difficult. I've grown quite used to these little games of hers."

"But why should she tell stories like that?"

"Why?" Sachiko shrugged. "It's just what children like to do. Once you become a mother, Etsuko, you'll need to get used to such things."

"You're sure she was with no one tonight?"

"Quite sure. I know my own daughter well enough."

We fell silent for a moment. Mosquitoes were humming in the air around us. Sachiko gave a yawn, covering her mouth with a hand.

"So you see, Etsuko," she said, "I'll be leaving Japan very shortly. You don't seem very impressed."

"Of course I am. And I'm very pleased, if this is what you wished. But won't there be . . . various difficulties?"

"Difficulties?"

"I mean, moving to a different country, with a different language and foreign ways."

"I understand your concern, Etsuko. But really, I don't think there's much for me to worry about. You see, I've heard so much about America, it won't be like an entirely foreign country. And as for the language, I already speak it to a certain extent. Frank-San and I, we always talk in English. Once I've been in America for a little while, I should speak it like an American woman. I really don't see there's any cause for me to be worrying. I know I'll manage."

43

I gave a small bow, but said nothing. Two of the kittens began making their way towards where Sachiko was sitting. She watched them for a moment, then gave a laugh. "Of course," she said, "I sometimes have moments when I wonder how everything will turn out. But really" — she smiled at me — "I know I'll manage."

"Actually," I said, "it was Mariko I had in mind. What will become of her?"

"Mariko? Oh, she'll be fine. You know how children are. They find it so much easier to settle into new surroundings, don't they?"

"But it would still be an enormous change for her. Is she ready for such a thing?"

Sachiko sighed impatiently. "Really, Etsuko, did you think I hadn't considered all this? Did you suppose I would decide to leave the country without having first given the most careful consideration to my daughter's welfare?"

"Naturally," I said, "you'd give it the most careful consideration."

"My daughter's welfare is of the utmost importance to me, Etsuko. I wouldn't make any decision that jeopardized her future. I've given the whole matter much consideration, and I've discussed it with Frank. I assure you, Mariko will be fine. There'll be no problems."

"But her education, what will become of that?"

Sachiko laughed again. "Etsuko, I'm not about to leave for the jungle. There are such things as schools in America. And you must understand, my daughter is a very bright child. Her father was an accomplished man, and on my side too, there were relatives of the highest rank. You mustn't suppose, Etsuko, simply because you've seen her in these . . . in these present surroundings, that she's some peasant's child."

"Of course not. I didn't for one moment . . . "

"She's a very bright child. You haven't seen her as she really is, Etsuko. In surroundings like this, you can only

44

expect a child to prove a little awkward at times. But if you'd seen her while we were at my uncle's house, you'd have seen her true qualities then. If an adult addressed her, she'd answer back very clearly and intelligently, there'd be none of this giggling and shying away like most other children. And there were certainly none of these little games of hers. She went to school, and made friends with the best kinds of children. And we had a private tutor for her, and he praised her very highly. It was astonishing how quickly she began to catch up."

"To catch up?"

"Well" — Sachiko gave a shrug — "it's unfortunate that Mariko's education's had to be interrupted from time to time. What with one thing and another, and our moving around so much. But these are difficult times we've come through, Etsuko. If it wasn't for the war, if my husband was still alive, then Mariko would have had the kind of up-bringing appropriate to a family of our position."

"Yes," I said. "Indeed."

Perhaps Sachiko had caught something in my tone; she looked up and stared at me, and when she spoke again, her voice had become more tense.

"I didn't need to leave Tokyo, Etsuko," she said. "But I did, for Mariko's sake. I came all this way to stay at my uncle's house, because I thought it would be best for my daughter. I didn't have to do that, I didn't need to leave Tokyo at all."

I gave a bow. Sachiko looked at me for a moment, then turned and gazed out through the open partitions, out into the darkness.

"But you've left your uncle now," I said. "And now you're about to leave Japan."

Sachiko glared at me angrily. "Why do you speak to me like this, Etsuko? Why is it you can't wish me well? Is it simply that you're envious?"

"But I do wish you well. And I assure you I . . ."

45

"Mariko will be fine in America, why won't you believe that? It's a better place for a child to grow up. And she'll have far more opportunities there, life's much better for a woman in America."

"I assure you I'm happy for you. As for myself, I couldn't be happier with things as they are. Jiro's work is going so well, and now the child arriving just when we wanted it . . ."

"She could become a business girl, a film actress even. America's like that, Etsuko, so many things are possible. Frank says I could become a business woman too. Such things are possible out there."

"I'm sure they are. It's just that personally, I'm very happy with my life where I am."

Sachiko gazed at the two small kittens, clawing at the tatami beside her. For several moments we were silent.

"I must be getting back," I said, eventually. "They'll be getting worried about me." I rose to my feet, but Sachiko did not take her eyes off the kittens. "When is it you leave?" I asked.

"Within the next few days. Frank will come and get us in his car. We should be on a ship by the end of the week."

"I take it then you won't be helping Mrs Fujiwara much longer."

Sachiko looked up at me with a short incredulous laugh. "Etsuko, I'm about to go to America. There's no need for me to work any more in a noodle shop."

"I see."

"In fact, Etsuko, perhaps you'd care to tell Mrs Fujiwara what's happened to me. I don't expect to be seeing her again."

"Won't you tell her yourself?"

She sighed impatiently. "Etsuko, can't you appreciate how loathsome it's been for someone such as myself to work each day in a noodle shop? But I didn't complain and I did what was required of me. But now it's over, I've no

46

great wish to see that place again." A kitten had been clawing at the sleeve of Sachiko's kimono. She gave it a sharp slap with the back of her hand and the little creature went scurrying back across the tatami. "So please give my regards to Mrs Fujiwara," she said. "And my best wishes for her trade."

"I'll do that. Now please excuse me, I must go."

This time, Sachiko got to her feet and accompanied me to the entryway.

"I'll come and say goodbye before we leave," she said, as I was putting on my sandals.

At first it had seemed a perfectly innocent dream; I had merely dreamt of something I had seen the previous day — the little girl we had watched playing in the park. And then the dream came back the following night. Indeed, over the past few months, it has returned to me several times.

Niki and I had watched the girl playing on the swings the afternoon we had walked into the village. It was the third day of Niki's visit and the rain had eased to a drizzle. I had not been out of the house for several days and enjoyed the feel of the air as we stepped into the winding lane outside.

Niki tended to walk rather fast, her narrow leather boots creaking with each stride. Although I found it no trouble keeping up with her, I would have preferred a more leisurely pace. Niki, one supposes, has yet to learn the pleasures of walking for its own sake. Neither does she seem sensitive to the feel of the countryside despite having grown up here. I said as much to her as we walked, and she retorted that this was not the real countryside, just a residential version to cater for the wealthy people who lived here. I dare say she is right; I have never ventured north to the agricultural areas of England where, Niki insists, I will find the real countryside. Nevertheless, there is a calm and quietness about these lanes I have come to

47

appreciate over the years.

When we arrived at the village I took Niki to the tea shop where I sometimes go. The village is small, just a few hotels and shops; the tea shop is on a street corner, upstairs above a bakery. That afternoon, Niki and I sat at a table next to the windows, and it was from there we watched the little girl playing in the park below. As we watched, she climbed on to a swing and called out towards two women sitting together on a bench nearby. She was a cheerful little girl, dressed in a green mackintosh and small Wellington boots.

"Perhaps you'll get married and have children soon," I said. "I miss little children."

"I can't think of anything I'd like less," said Niki.

"Well, I suppose you're still rather young."

"It's nothing to do with how young or old I am. I just don't feel like having a lot of kids screaming around me."

"Don't worry, Niki," I said, with a laugh. "I wasn't insisting you became a mother just yet. I had this passing fancy just now to be a grandmother, that's all. I thought perhaps you'd oblige, but it can wait."

The little girl, standing on the seat of the swing, was pulling hard on the chains, but somehow she could not make the swing go higher. She smiled anyway and called out again to the women.

"A friend of mine's just had a baby," Niki said. "She's really pleased. I can't think why. Horrible screaming thing she's produced."

"Well, at least she's happy. How old is your friend?"

"Nineteen."

"Nineteen? She's even younger than you are. Is she married?"

"No. What difference does that make?"

"But surely she can't be happy about it."

"Why not? Just because she isn't married?"

"There's that. And the fact that she's only nineteen. I can't believe she was happy about it."

48

"What difference does it make whether she's married? She wanted it, she planned it and everything."

"Is that what she told you?"

"But, Mother, I know her, she's a friend of mine. I know she wanted it."

The women on the bench got to their feet. One of them called to the little girl. She came off the swing and went running towards the women.

"And what about the father?" I asked.

"He was happy about it too. I remember when they first found out. We all went out to celebrate."

"But people always pretend to be delighted. It's like that film we saw on the television last night."

"What film?"

"I expect you weren't watching it. You were reading your magazine."

"Oh that. It looked awful."

"It certainly was. But that's what I mean. I'm sure nobody ever receives the news of a baby like these people do in these films."

"Honestly, Mother, I don't know how you can sit and watch rubbish like that. You hardly used to watch television at all. I remember you used to keep telling me off because I watched it so much."

I laughed. "You see how our roles are reversing, Niki. I'm sure you're very good for me. You must stop me wasting my time away like that."

As we made our way back from the tea shop, the sky had clouded over ominously and the drizzle had become heavier. We had walked a little way past the small railway station when a voice called from behind us: "Mrs Sheringham! Mrs Sheringham!"

I turned and saw a small woman in an overcoat hurrying up the road.

"I thought it was you," she said, catching up with us.

49

"And how have you been keeping?" She gave me a cheerful smile.

"Hello, Mrs Waters," I said. "How nice to see you again."

"Seems to have turned all miserable again, hasn't it? Why, hello, Keiko" — she touched Niki's sleeve — "I didn't realize it was you."

"No," I said hurriedly, "this is Niki."

"Niki, of course. Good gracious, you've completely grown up, dear. That's why I got you muddled. You've completely grown up."

"Hello, Mrs Waters," Niki said, recovering.

Mrs Waters lives not far from me. These days I see her only very occasionally, but several years ago she had given piano lessons to both my daughters. She had taught Keiko for a number of years, and then Niki for a year or so when she was still a child. It had not taken me long to see Mrs Waters was a very limited pianist and her attitude to music in general had often irritated me; for instance, she would refer to works by Chopin and Tchaikovsky alike as "charming melodies". But she was such an affectionate woman I never had the heart to replace her.

"And what are you doing with yourself these days, dear?" she asked Niki.

"Me? Oh, I live in London."

"Oh yes? And what are you doing there? Studying?"

"I'm not doing anything really. I just live there."

"Oh, I see. But you're happy there, are you? That's the main thing, isn't it."

"Yes, I'm happy enough."

"Well, that's the main thing, isn't it. And what about Keiko?" Mrs Waters turned to me. "How is Keiko getting on now?"

"Keiko? Oh, she went to live in Manchester."

"Oh yes? That's a nice city on the whole. That's what I've heard anyway. And does she like it up there?"

"I haven't heard from her recently."

"Oh well. No news is good news, I expect. And does Keiko still play the piano?"

"I expect she does. I haven't heard from her recently."

My lack of enthusiasm seemed finally to penetrate, and she dropped the subject with an awkward laugh. Such persistence on her part has characterized our encounters over the years since Keiko's leaving home. Neither my evident reluctance to discuss Keiko nor the fact that until that afternoon I had been unable to tell her so much as my daughter's whereabouts had succeeded in making any lasting impression upon her. In all probability, Mrs Waters will continue to ask cheerfully after my daughter whenever we happen to meet.

By the time we got home, the rain was falling steadily.

"I suppose I embarrassed you, didn't I?" Niki said to me. We were sitting once again in our armchairs, looking out into the garden.

"Why do you suppose that?" I said.

"I should have told her I was thinking of going to university or something like that."

"I don't mind in the least what you say about yourself. I'm not ashamed of you."

"No, I suppose not."

"But I did think you were rather off-hand with her. You never did like that woman much, did you?"

"Mrs Waters? Well, I used to hate those lessons she gave me. They were sheer boredom. I used to just go off in a dream, then now and again there'd be this little voice telling me to put my finger here or here or here. Was that your idea, getting me to have lessons?"

"It was mainly mine. You see, I had great plans for you once."

Niki laughed. "I'm sorry to be such a failure. But it's your own fault. I haven't got any musical sense at all. There's this girl in our house who plays the guitar, and she was trying to

51

show me some chords, but I couldn't be bothered to even learn those. I think Mrs Waters put me off music for life."

"You may come back to it some time and you'll appreciate having had lessons."

"But I've forgotten everything I ever learnt."

"I doubt if you would have forgotten everything. Nothing you learn at that age is totally lost."

"A waste of time, anyway," Niki muttered. She sat looking out of the windows for some time. Then she turned to me and said: "I suppose it must be quite difficult to tell people. About Keiko, I mean."

"It seemed easiest to say what I did," I replied. "She rather took me by surprise."

"Yes, I suppose so." Niki went on looking out of the window with an empty expression. "Keiko didn't come to Dad's funeral, did she?" she said, eventually.

"You know perfectly well she didn't so why ask?"

"I was just saying, that's all."

"You mean you didn't come to her funeral because she didn't come to your father's? Don't be so childish, Niki."

"I'm not being childish. I'm just saying that's the way it was. She was never a part of our lives — not mine or Dad's anyway. I never expected her to be at Dad's funeral."

I did not reply and we sat silently in our armchairs. Then Niki said:

"It was odd just now, with Mrs Waters. It was almost like you enjoyed it."

"Enjoyed what?"

"Pretending Keiko was alive."

"I don't enjoy deceiving people." Perhaps I snapped a little, for Niki looked startled.

"No, I suppose not," she said, lamely.

It rained throughout that night, and the next day — the fourth day of Niki's stay — it was still raining steadily.

"Do you mind if I change rooms tonight?" Niki said. "I could use the spare bedroom." We were in the kitchen, washing the dishes after breakfast.

"The spare bedroom?" I laughed a little. "They're all spare bedrooms now. No, there's no reason why you shouldn't sleep in the spare room. Have you taken a dislike to your old room?"

"I feel a bit odd sleeping there."

"How unkind, Niki. I hoped you'd still feel it was your room."

"Yes, I do," she said, hurriedly. "It's not that I don't like it." She fell silent, wiping some knives with a tea-towel. Finally she said: "It's that other room. Her room. It gives me an odd feeling, that room being right opposite."

I stopped what I was doing and looked at her sternly.

"Well, I can't help it, Mother. I just feel strange thinking about that room being right opposite."

"Take the spare room by all means," I said, coldly. "But you'll need to make up the bed in there."

Although I had made a show of being upset by Niki's request to change rooms, I had no wish to make it difficult for her to do so. For I too had experienced a disturbing feeling about that room opposite. In many ways, that room is the most pleasant in the house, with a splendid view across the orchard. But it had been Keiko's fanatically guarded domain for so long, a strange spell seemed to linger there even now, six years after she had left it — a spell that had grown all the stronger now that Keiko was dead.

For the two or three years before she finally left us, Keiko had retreated into that bedroom, shutting us out of her life. She rarely came out, although I would sometimes hear her moving around the house after we had all gone to bed. I surmised that she spent her time reading magazines and listening to her radio. She had no friends, and the rest of us were forbidden entry into her room. At mealtimes I would

53

leave her plate in the kitchen and she would come down to get it, then shut herself in again. The room, I realized, was in a terrible condition. An odour of stale perfume and dirty linen came from within, and on the occasions I had glimpsed inside, I had seen countless glossy magazines lying on the floor amidst heaps of clothes. I had to coax her to put out her laundry, and in this at least we reached an understanding: every few weeks I would find a bag of washing outside her door, which I would wash and return. In the end, the rest of us grew used to her ways, and when by some impulse Keiko ventured down into our living room, we would all feel a great tension. Invariably, these excursions would end with her fighting, with Niki or with my husband, and then she would be back in her room.

I never saw Keiko's room in Manchester, the room in which she died. It may seem morbid of a mother to have such thoughts, but on hearing of her suicide, the first thought that ran through my mind — before I registered even the shock — was to wonder how long she had been there like that before they had found her. She had lived amidst her own family without being seen for days on end; little hope she would be discovered quickly in a strange city where no one knew her. Later, the coroner said she had been there "for several days". It was the landlady who had opened the door, thinking Keiko had left without paying the rent.

I have found myself continually bringing to mind that picture — of my daughter hanging in her room for days on end. The horror of that image has never diminished, but it has long ceased to be a morbid matter; as with a wound on one's own body, it is possible to develop an intimacy with the most disturbing of things.

"I'll probably be warmer in the spare room anyhow," Niki said.

"If you're cold at night, Niki, you can simply turn up the heating."

"I suppose so." She gave a sigh. "I haven't slept very well lately. I think I'm getting bad dreams, but I can never remember them properly once I wake up."

"I had a dream last night," I said.

"I think it might be to do with the quiet. I'm not used to it being so quiet at night."

"I dreamt about that little girl. The one we were watching yesterday. The little girl in the park."

"I can sleep right through traffic, but I've forgotten what it's like, sleeping in the quiet." Niki shrugged and dropped some cutlery into the drawer. "Perhaps I'll sleep better in the spare room."

The fact that I mentioned my dream to Niki, that first time I had it, indicates perhaps that I had doubts even then as to its innocence. I must have suspected from the start — without fully knowing why — that the dream had to do not so much with the little girl we had watched, but with my having remembered Sachiko two days previously.

Chapter Four

I was in the kitchen one afternoon preparing the supper before my husband came home from work, when I heard a strange sound coming from the living room. I stopped what I was doing and listened. It came again — the sound of a violin being played very badly. The noises continued for a few minutes then stopped.

When eventually I went into the living room, I found Ogata-San bowed over a chess-board. The late afternoon sun was streaming in and despite the electric fans a humidity had set in all around the apartment. I opened the windows a little wider.

"Didn't you finish your game last night?" I asked, coming over to him.

"No, Jiro claimed he was too tired. A ploy on his part, I suspect. You see, I have him in a nice corner here."

"I see."

"He's relying on the fact that my memory's so foggy these days. So I'm just going over my strategy again."

"How resourceful of you, Father. But I doubt if Jiro's mind works quite so cunningly."

"Perhaps not. I dare say you know him better than I do these days." Ogata-San continued to study the board for several moments, then looked up and laughed. "This must seem amusing to you. Jiro sweating away in his office and here I am preparing a game of chess for when he comes home. I feel like a small child waiting for his father."

"Well, I'd much rather you occupied yourself with chess. Your musical recital earlier was hideous."

"How disrespectful. And I thought you'd be moved, Etsuko."

The violin was on the floor nearby, put back in its case. Ogata-San watched me as I began opening the case.

"I noticed it up there on the shelf," he said. "I took the liberty of bringing it down. Don't look so concerned, Etsuko. I was very gentle with it."

"I can't be sure. As you say, Father's like a child these days." I held up the violin and examined it. "Except small children can't reach up to high shelves."

I tucked the instrument under my chin. Ogata-San continued to watch me.

"Play something for me," he said. "I'm sure you can do better than me."

"I'm sure I can." Once more I held the violin out at arm's length. "But it's been such a long time."

"You mean you haven't been practising? Now that's a pity, Etsuko. You used to be so devoted to the instrument."

"I suppose I was once. But I hardly touch it now."

"A great shame, Etsuko. And you were so devoted. I remember when you used to play in the dead of night and wake up the house."

"Wake up the house? When did I do that?"

"Yes, I remember. When you first came to stay with us." Ogata-San gave a laugh. "Don't look so worried, Etsuko. We all forgave you. Now let me see, who was the composer you used to admire so much? Was it Mendelssohn?"

"Is that true? I woke up the house?"

"Don't look so worried, Etsuko. It was years ago. Play me something by Mendelssohn."

"But why didn't you stop me?"

"It was only for the first few nights. And besides, we didn't mind in the least."

I plucked the strings lightly. The violin was out of tune.

"I must have been such a burden to you in those days," I said, quietly.

"Nonsense."

"But the rest of the family. They must have thought I was

57

a mad girl."

"They couldn't have thought too badly of you. After all, it ended up with you marrying Jiro. Now come on, Etsuko, enough of this. Play me something."

"What was I like in those days, Father? Was I like a mad person?"

"You were very shocked, which was only to be expected. We were all shocked, those of us who were left. Now, Etsuko, let's forget these things. I'm sorry I ever brought up the matter."

I brought the instrument up to my chin once more.

"Ah," he said, "Mendelssohn."

I remained like that for several seconds, the violin under my chin. Then I brought it down to my lap and sighed. "I hardly play it now," I said.

"I'm sorry, Etsuko." Ogata-San's voice had become solemn. "Perhaps I shouldn't have touched it."

I looked up at him and smiled. "So," I said, "the little child is feeling guilty now."

"It's just that I saw it up there and I remembered it from those days."

"I'll play it for you another time. After I've practised a little."

He gave me a small bow, and the smile returned to his eyes.

"I'll remember you promised, Etsuko. And perhaps you could teach me a little."

"I can't teach you everything, Father. You said you wanted to learn to cook."

"Ah yes. That too."

"I'll play for you the next time you come to stay with us."

"I'll remember you promised," he said.

After supper that evening, Jiro and his father settled down to their game of chess. I cleared up the supper things and

58

then sat down with some sewing. At one point during their game, Ogata-San said:

"I've just noticed something. If you don't mind, I'd like to make that move again."

"Certainly," said Jiro.

"But then it's rather unfair on you. Especially since I seem to have the better of you at the moment."

"No, not at all. Please take the move again."

"You don't mind?"

"Not at all."

They played on in silence.

"Jiro," Ogata-San said after several minutes, "I was just wondering. Have you written that letter yet? To Shigeo Matsuda?"

I looked up from my sewing. Jiro appeared absorbed in the game and did not reply until he had moved his piece. "Shigeo? Well, not yet. I've been meaning to. But I've been so busy just recently."

"Of course. I quite understand. I just happened to think of it, that's all."

"I don't seem to have had much time just recently."

"Of course. There's no hurry. I don't mean to keep pestering you like this. It's just that it might be more appropriate if he heard from you fairly soon. It's a few weeks now since his article appeared."

"Yes, certainly. You're quite right."

They returned to their game. For some moments neither of them spoke. Then Ogata-San said:

"How do you suppose he'll react?"

"Shigeo? I don't know. As I say, I don't know him very well these days."

"He's joined the Communist Party, you say?"

"I'm not certain. He certainly expressed such sympathies when I last saw him."

"A great pity. But then there are so many things in Japan today to sway a young man."

"Yes, no doubt."

"So many young men these days get carried away with ideas and theories. But perhaps he'll back down and apologize. There's nothing like a timely reminder of one's personal obligations. You know, I suspect Shigeo never even stopped to consider what he was doing. I think he wrote that article with a pen in one hand and his books about communism in the other. He may well back down in the end."

"Quite possibly. I've just had so much work recently."

"Of course, of course. Your work must take precedence. Please don't worry about it. Now, was it my move?"

They continued their game, speaking little. Once I heard Ogata-San say: "You're moving just as I anticipated. You'll need to be very clever to escape from that corner."

They had been playing for sometime when there was a knock at the door. Jiro looked up and threw me a glance. I put down my sewing and got to my feet.

When I opened the door, I found two men grinning and bowing at me. It was quite late by then and I thought at first they had come to the wrong apartment. But then I recognized them as two of Jiro's colleagues and asked them in. They stood in the entryway giggling to themselves. One was a tubby little man whose face looked quite flushed. His companion was thinner, with a pale complexion like that of a European; but it seemed he too had been drinking, for pink blotches had appeared on each of his cheeks. They were both wearing ties, loosened untidily, and were holding jackets over their arms.

Jiro seemed pleased to see them and called to them to sit down. But they remained in the entryway, giggling.

"Ah, Ogata," the pale-faced man said to Jiro, "perhaps we've caught you at a bad time."

"Not at all. What are you doing in these parts anyway?"

"We've been to see Murasaki's brother. In fact, we haven't been home yet."

"We came to disturb you because we're afraid to go home," the tubby man put in. "We didn't tell our wives we'd be late."

"What rabble you are, the pair of you," said Jiro. "Why don't you take off your shoes and come up here?"

"We've caught you at a bad time," the pale-faced man said again. "I can see you've got a visitor." He grinned and bowed towards Ogata-San.

"This is my father, but how can I introduce you if you don't come in?"

The visitors finally took off their shoes and seated themselves. Jiro introduced them to his father and they began once more to bow and giggle.

"You gentlemen are from Jiro's firm?" Ogata-San asked.

"Yes, indeed," the tubby man replied. "A great honour it is too, even if he does give us a tough time. We call your son 'Pharaoh' in the office because he urges the rest of us to work like slaves while he does nothing himself."

"What nonsense," said my husband.

"It's true. He orders us around like we're his dogsbodies. Then he sits down and reads the newspaper."

Ogata-San seemed a little confused, but seeing the others laugh he joined in.

"And what's this here?" The pale-faced man indicated the chess-board. "You see, I knew we'd interrupted something."

"We were just playing chess to pass the time," said Jiro.

"Go on playing then. Don't let rabble like us interrupt."

"Don't be silly. How could I concentrate with idiots like you around." Jiro pushed away the chess-board. One or two of the pieces fell over and he stood them up again without looking at the squares. "So. You've been to see Murasaki's brother. Etsuko, get some tea for the gentlemen." My husband had said this despite the fact that I was already on my way to the kitchen. But then the tubby man started to wave his hand frantically.

61

"Madam, madam, sit down. Please. We'll be going in just a moment. Please be seated."

"It's no trouble," I said, smiling.

"No, madam, I implore you" — he had started to shout quite loudly — "We're just rabble, like your husband says. Please don't make a fuss, please sit down."

I was about to obey him, but then I saw Jiro give me an angry look.

"At least have some tea with us," I said. "It's no trouble at all."

"Now you've sat down, you may as well stay a while," my husband said to the visitors. "Anyway, I want to know about Murasaki's brother. Is he as mad as they say he is?"

"He's a character all right," the tubby man said, with a laugh. "We certainly weren't disappointed. And did anyone tell you about his wife?"

I bowed and made my way into the kitchen unnoticed. I prepared the tea and put on to a plate some cakes I had been making earlier that day. I could hear laughter coming from the living room, my husband's voice amongst them. One of the visitors was calling him "Pharaoh" again in a loud voice. When I returned to the living room, Jiro and his visitors seemed in high spirits. The tubby man was relating an anecdote, about some cabinet minister's encounter with General MacArthur. I put the cakes near them, poured out their tea, then sat down beside Ogata-San. Jiro's friends made several more jokes concerning politicians and then the pale-faced man pretended to be offended because his companion had spoken disparagingly of some personage he admired. He kept a straight face while the others teased him.

"By the way, Hanada," my husband said to him. "I heard an interesting story the other day at the office. I was told during the last elections, you threatened to beat your wife with a golf club because she wouldn't vote the way you wanted."

"Where did you pick up this rubbish?"

"I got it from reliable sources."

"That's right," the tubby man said. "And your wife was going to call the police to report political intimidation."

"What rubbish. Besides, I don't have golf clubs any more. I sold them all last year."

"You still have that seven-iron," said the tubby man. "I saw it in your apartment last week. Maybe you used that."

"But you can't deny it, can you, Hanada?" said Jiro.

"It's nonsense about the golf club."

"But it's true you couldn't get her to obey you."

The pale-faced man shrugged. "Well, it's her personal right to vote any way she pleases."

"Then why did you threaten her?" his friend asked.

"I was trying to make her see sense, of course. My wife votes for Yoshida just because he looks like her uncle. That's typical of women. They don't understand politics. They think they can choose the country's leaders the same way they choose dresses."

"So you gave her a seven-iron," said Jiro.

"Is that really true?" Ogata-San asked. He had not spoken since I had come back in with the tea. The other three stopped laughing and the pale-faced man looked at Ogata-San with a surprised expression.

"Well, no." He became suddenly formal and gave a small bow. "I didn't actually hit her."

"No, no," said Ogata-San. "I meant your wife and yourself — you voted for separate parties?"

"Well, yes." He shrugged, then giggled awkwardly. "What could I do?"

"I'm sorry. I didn't mean to pry." Ogata-San gave a low bow, and the pale-faced man returned it. As if the bowing were a signal, the three younger men started once more to laugh and talk amongst themselves. They moved off politics and began discussing various members of their firm. When I was pouring more tea, I noticed that the cakes, despite my having put out a generous amount, had almost all disappeared. I finished refilling their teacups, then sat down again beside Ogata-San.

The visitors stayed for an hour or so. Jiro saw them to the door then sat down again with a sigh. "It's getting late," he said. "I'll need to turn in soon."

Ogata-San was examining the chess board. "I think the pieces got jogged a little," he said. "I'm sure the horse was on this square, not that one."

"Quite probably."

"I'll put it here then. Are we agreed on this?"

"Yes, yes, I'm sure you're right. We'll have to finish the game another time, Father. I'll need to retire very shortly."

"How about playing just the next few moves. We may well finish it off."

"Really, I'd rather not. I'm feeling very tired now."

"Of course."

I packed away the sewing I had been doing earlier in the evening and sat waiting for the others to retire. Jiro, however, picked up a newspaper and started to read the back page. Then he took the last remaining cake from the plate and began to eat nonchalantly. After several moments, Ogata-San said:

"Perhaps we ought to just finish it off now. It'll only take a few more moves."

"Father, I really am too tired now. I have work to go to in the morning."

"Yes, of course."

Jiro went back to his newspapers. He continued to eat the cake and I watched several crumbs drop on to the tatami. Ogata-San continued to gaze at the chess-board for some time.

"Quite extraordinary", he said, eventually, "what your friend was saying."

"Oh? What was that?" Jiro did not look up from his newspaper.

"About him and his wife voting for different parties. A few years ago that would have been unthinkable."

"No doubt."

"Quite extraordinary the things that happen now. But that's what's meant by democracy, I suppose." Ogata-San gave a sigh. "These things we've learnt so eagerly from the Americans, they aren't always to the good."

"No, indeed they're not."

"Look what happens. Husband and wife voting for different parties. It's a sad state of affairs when a wife can't be relied on in such matters any more."

Jiro continued to read his newspaper. "Yes, it's regrettable," he said.

"A wife these days feels no sense of loyalty towards the household. She just does what she pleases, votes for a different party if the whim takes her. That's so typical of the way things have gone in Japan. All in the name of democracy people abandon obligations."

Jiro looked up at his father for a brief moment, then turned his eyes back to his paper. "No doubt you're very right," he said. "But surely the Americans didn't bring all bad."

"The Americans, they never understood the way things were in Japan. Not for one moment have they understood. Their ways may be fine for Americans, but in Japan things are different, very different." Ogata-San sighed again. "Discipline, loyalty, such things held Japan together once. That may sound fanciful, but it's true. People were bound by a sense of duty. Towards one's family, towards superiors, towards the country. But now instead there's all this talk of democracy. You hear it whenever people want to be selfish, whenever they want to forget obligations."

"Yes, no doubt you're right." Jiro yawned and scratched the side of his face.

65

"Take what happened in my profession, for instance. Here was a system we'd nurtured and cherished for years. The Americans came and stripped it, tore it down without a thought. They decided our schools would be like American schools, the children should learn what American children learn. And the Japanese welcomed it all. Welcomed it with a lot of talk about democracy" — he shook his head — "Many fine things were destroyed in our schools."

"Yes, I'm sure that's very true." Jiro glanced up once more. "But surely there were some faults in the old system, in schools as much as anywhere."

"Jiro, what is this? Something you read somewhere?"

"It's just my opinion."

"Did you read that in your newspaper? I devoted my life to the teaching of the young. And then I watched the Americans tear it all down. Quite extraordinary what goes on in schools now, the way children are taught to behave. Extraordinary. And so much just isn't taught any more. Do you know, children leave school today knowing nothing about the history of their own country?"

"That may be a pity, admittedly. But then I remember some odd things from my schooldays. I remember being taught all about how Japan was created by the gods, for instance. How we as a nation were divine and supreme. We had to memorize the text book word for word. Some things aren't such a loss, perhaps."

"But Jiro, things aren't as simple as that. You clearly don't understand how such things worked. Things aren't nearly as simple as you presume. We devoted ourselves to ensuring that proper qualities were handed down, that children grew up with the correct attitude to their country, to their fellows. There was a spirit in Japan once, it bound us all together. Just imagine what it must be like being a young boy today. He's taught no values at school — except perhaps that he should selfishly demand whatever he wants out of life. He goes home and finds his parents

66

fighting because his mother refuses to vote for his father's party. What a state of affairs."

"Yes, I see your point. Now, Father, I'm sorry but I must go to bed."

"We did our best, men like Endo and I, we did our best to nurture what was good in the country. A lot of good has been destroyed."

"It's most regrettable." My husband got to his feet. "Excuse me, Father, but I must sleep. I have another busy day tomorrow."

Ogata-San looked up at his son, a somewhat surprised expression on his face. "Why, of course. How inconsiderate of me to have kept you so late." He gave a small bow.

"Not at all. I'm sorry we can't talk longer, but I really ought to get some sleep now."

"Why, of course."

Jiro wished his father a good night's sleep and left the room. For a few seconds, Ogata-San gazed at the door through which Jiro had disappeared as if he expected his son to return at any moment. Then he turned to me with a troubled look.

"I didn't realize how late it was," he said. "I didn't mean to keep Jiro up."

Chapter Five

"Gone? And had he left you no message at his hotel?"

Sachiko laughed. "You look so astonished, Etsuko," she said. "No, he'd left nothing. He'd gone yesterday morning, that's all they knew. To tell you the truth, I half expected this."

I realized I was still holding the tray. I laid it down carefully then seated myself on a cushion opposite Sachiko. There was a pleasant breeze blowing through the apartment that morning.

"But how terrible for you," I said. "And you were waiting with everything packed and ready."

"This is nothing new to me, Etsuko. Back in Tokyo — that's where I first met him, you see — back in Tokyo, it was just the same thing. Oh no, this is nothing new to me. I've learnt to expect such things."

"And you say you're going back into town tonight? On your own?"

"Don't look so shocked, Etsuko. After Tokyo, Nagasaki seems a tame little town. If he's still in Nagasaki, I'll find him tonight. He may change his hotel, but he won't have changed his habits."

"But this is all so distressing. If you wish, I'd be glad to come and sit with Mariko until you get back."

"Why, how kind of you. Mariko's quite capable of being left on her own, but if you're prepared to spend a couple of hours with her tonight, that would be most kind. But I'm sure this whole thing will sort itself out, Etsuko. You see, when you've come through some of the things I have, you learn not to let small set-backs like this worry you."

"But what if he's . . . I mean, what if he's left Nagasaki altogether?"

"Oh, he hasn't gone far, Etsuko. Besides, if he really meant to leave me, he would have left a note of some kind, wouldn't he? You see, he hasn't gone far. He knows I'll come and find him."

Sachiko looked at me and smiled. I found myself at a loss for any reply.

"Besides, Etsuko," she went on, "he did come all the way down here. He came down all this way to Nagasaki to find me at my uncle's house, all that way from Tokyo. Now why would he have done that if he didn't mean everything he's promised? You see, Etsuko, what he wants most is to take me to America. That's what he wants. Nothing's changed really, this is just a slight delay." She gave a quick laugh. "Sometimes, you see, he's like a little child."

"But what do you think your friend means by going off like this? I don't understand."

"There's nothing to understand, Etsuko, it hardly matters. What he really wants is to take me to America and lead a steady respectable life there. That's what he really wants. Otherwise why would he have come all that way and found me at my uncle's house? You see, Etsuko, this isn't anything to be so worried about."

"No, I'm sure it isn't."

Sachiko seemed about to speak again, but then appeared to stop herself. She stared down at the tea things on the tray. "Well then, Etsuko," she said, with a smile, "let's pour the tea."

She watched in silence as I poured. Once when I glanced quickly towards her, she smiled as if to encourage me. I finished pouring the tea and for a moment or two we sat there quietly.

"Incidentally, Etsuko," Sachiko said, "I take it you've spoken to Mrs Fujiwara and explained my position to her."

"Yes. I saw her the day before yesterday."

69

"I suppose she'd been wondering what had become of me."

"I explained to her that you'd been called away to America. She was perfectly understanding about it."

"You see, Etsuko," said Sachiko, "I find myself in a difficult situation now."

"Yes, I can appreciate that."

"As regards finances, as well as everything else."

"Yes, I see," I said, with a small bow. "If you wish, I could certainly talk to Mrs Fujiwara. I'm sure under the circumstances she'd be happy to . . ."

"No, no, Etsuko" — Sachiko gave a laugh — "I've no desire to return to her little noodle shop. I fully expect to be leaving for America in the near future. It's merely a case of things being delayed a little, that's all. But in the meantime, you see, I'll need a little money. And I was just remembering, Etsuko, how you once offered to assist me in that respect."

She was looking at me with a kindly smile. I looked back at her for a few moments. Then I bowed and said:

"I have some savings of my own. Not a great deal, but I'd be glad to do what I can."

Sachiko bowed gracefully, then lifted her teacup. "I won't embarrass you", she said, "by naming any particular sum. That, of course, is entirely up to you. I'll gratefully accept whatever you feel is appropriate. Of course, the loan will be returned in due course, you can rest assured of that, Etsuko."

"Naturally," I said, quietly. "I had no doubts on that."

Sachiko continued to regard me with her kindly smile. I excused myself and left the room.

In the bedroom, the sun was streaming in, revealing all the dust in the air. I knelt beside a set of small drawers at the foot of our cupboard. From the lowest drawer I removed various items — photograph albums, greeting cards, a folder of water-colours my mother had painted — laying them carefully on the floor beside me. At the bottom of the drawer was the black lacquer gift-box. Lifting the lid, I found the several letters I had preserved — unknown to my husband — together with two or three small photographs. From beneath these, I took out the envelope containing my money. I carefully put back everything as it had been and closed the drawer. Before leaving the room, I opened the wardrobe, chose a silk scarf of a suitably discreet pattern, and wrapped it around the envelope.

When I returned to the living room, Sachiko was refilling her teacup. She did not look up at me, and when I laid the folded scarf on the floor beside her, she carried on pouring the tea without glancing at it. She gave me a nod as I sat down, then began to sip from her cup. Only once, as she was lowering her teacup, did she cast a quick sideways glance at the bundle beside her cushion.

"There's something you don't seem to understand, Etsuko," she said. "You see, I'm not ashamed or embarrassed about anything I've done. You can feel free to ask whatever you like."

"Yes, of course."

"For instance, Etsuko, why is it you never ask me anything about 'my friend', as you insist on calling him? There really isn't anything to get embarrassed about. Why, Etsuko, you're beginning to blush already."

"I assure you I'm not getting embarrassed. In fact . . ."

"But you are, Etsuko, I can see you are." Sachiko gave a laugh and clapped her hands together. "But why can't you understand I've nothing to hide, I've nothing to be ashamed of? Why are you blushing like this? Just because I mentioned Frank?"

"But I'm not embarrassed. And I assure you I've never assumed anything . . ."

"Why do you never ask me about him, Etsuko? There must be all sorts of questions you'd like to ask. So why don't you ask them? After all, everybody else in the neigh-

71

bourhood seems interested enough, you must be too, Etsuko. So please feel free, ask me anything you like."

"But really, I . . ."

"Come on, Etsuko, I insist. Ask me about him. I do want you to. Ask me about him, Etsuko."

"Very well then."

"Well? Go on, Etsuko, ask."

"Very well. What does he look like, your friend?"

"What does he look like?" Sachiko laughed again. "Is that all you wish to know? Well, he's tall like most of these foreigners, and his hair's going a little thin. He's not old, you understand. Foreigners go bald more easily, did you know that, Etsuko? Now ask me something else about him. There must be other things you want to know."

"Well, quite honestly . . ."

"Come on, Etsuko, ask. I want you to ask."

"But really, there's nothing I wish to . . ."

"But there must be, why won't you ask? Ask me about him, Etsuko, ask me."

"Well, in fact," I said, "I did wonder about one thing."

Sachiko seemed to suddenly freeze. She had been holding her hands together in front of her, but now she lowered them and placed them back on her lap.

"I did wonder", I said, "if he spoke Japanese at all."

For a moment, Sachiko said nothing. Then she smiled and her manner seemed to relax. She lifted her teacup again and took several sips. Then when she spoke again, her voice sounded almost dreamy.

"Foreigners have so much trouble with our language," she said. She paused and smiled to herself. "Frank's Japanese is quite terrible, so we converse in English. Do you know English at all, Etsuko? Not at all? You see, my father used to speak good English. He had connections in Europe and he always used to encourage me to study the language. But then of course, when I married, I stopped learning. My husband forbade it. He took away all my

72

English books. But I didn't forget it. When I met foreigners in Tokyo, it came back to me."

We sat in silence for a little while. Then Sachiko gave a tired sigh.

"I suppose I'd better get back fairly soon," she said. She reached down and picked up the folded scarf. Then without inspecting it, she dropped it into her handbag.

"You won't have a little more tea?" I asked.

She shrugged. "Just a little more perhaps."

I refilled the cups. Sachiko watched me, then said: "If it's inconvenient — about tonight, I mean — it wouldn't matter at all. Mariko should be capable of being left on her own by now."

"It's no trouble. I'm sure my husband won't object."

"You're very kind, Etsuko," Sachiko said, in a flat tone. Then she said: "I should warn you, perhaps. My daughter has been in a somewhat difficult mood these past few days."

"That's all right," I said, smiling. "I'll need to get used to children in every kind of mood."

Sachiko went on drinking her tea slowly. She seemed in no hurry to be returning. Then she put down her teacup and for some moments sat examining the back of her hands.

"I know it was a terrible thing that happened here in Nagasaki," she said, finally. "But it was bad in Tokyo too. Week after week it went on, it was very bad. Towards the end we were all living in tunnels and derelict buildings and there was nothing but rubble. Everyone who lived in Tokyo saw unpleasant things. And Mariko did too." She continued to gaze at the back of her hands.

"Yes," I said. "It must have been a very difficult time."

"This woman. This woman you've heard Mariko talk about. That was something Mariko saw in Tokyo. She saw other things in Tokyo, some terrible things, but she's always remembered that woman." She turned over her hands and looked at the palms looking from one to the other as if to compare them.

"And this woman," I said. "She was killed in an air-raid?"

"She killed herself. They said she cut her throat. I never knew her. You see, Mariko went running off one morning. I can't remember why, perhaps she was upset about something. Anyway she went running off out into the streets, so I went chasing after her. It was very early, there was nobody about. Mariko ran down an alleyway, and I followed after her. There was a canal at the end and the woman was kneeling there, up to her elbows in water. A young woman, very thin. I knew something was wrong as soon as I saw her. You see, Etsuko, she turned round and smiled at Mariko. I knew something was wrong and Mariko must have done too because she stopped running. At first I thought the woman was blind, she had that kind of look, her eyes didn't seem to actually see anything. Well, she brought her arms out of the canal and showed us what she'd been holding under the water. It was a baby. I took hold of Mariko then and we came out of the alley."

I remained silent, waiting for her to continue. Sachiko helped herself to more tea from the pot.

"As I say," she said, "I heard the woman killed herself. That was a few days afterwards."

"How old was Mariko then?"

"Five, almost six. She saw other things in Tokyo. But she always remembers that woman."

"She saw everything? She saw the baby?"

"Yes. Actually, for a long time I thought she hadn't understood what she'd seen. She didn't talk about it afterwards. She didn't even seem particularly upset at the time. She didn't start talking about it until a month or so later. We were sleeping in this old building then. I woke up in the night and saw Mariko sitting up, staring at the doorway. There wasn't a door, it was just this doorway, and Mariko

74

was sitting up looking at it. I was quite alarmed. You see, there was nothing to stop anyone walking into the building. I asked Mariko what was wrong and she said a woman had been standing there watching us. I asked what sort of woman and Mariko said it was the one we'd seen that morning. Watching us from the doorway. I got up and looked around but there wasn't anyone there. It's quite possible, of course, that some woman was standing there. There was nothing to stop anyone stepping inside."

"I see. And Mariko mistook her for the woman you'd seen."

"I expect that's what happened. In any case, that's when it started, Mariko's obsession with that woman. I thought she'd grown out of it, but just recently it's started again. If she starts to talk about it tonight, please don't pay her any attention."

"Yes, I see."

"You know how it is with children," said Sachiko. "They play at make-believe and they get confused where their fantasies begin and end."

"Yes, I suppose it's nothing unusual really."

"You see, Etsuko, things were very difficult when Mariko was born."

"Yes, they must have been," I said. "I'm very fortunate, I know."

"Things were very difficult. Perhaps it was foolish to have married when I did. After all, everyone could see a war was coming. But then again, Etsuko, no one knew what a war was really like, not in those days. I married into a highly respected family. I never thought a war could change things so much."

Sachiko put down her teacup and passed a hand through her hair. Then she smiled quickly. "As regards tonight, Etsuko," she said, "my daughter is quite capable of amusing herself. So please don't bother too much with her."

Mrs Fujiwara's face often grew weary when she talked about her son.

"He's becoming an old man," she was saying. "Soon he'll have only the old maids to choose from."

We were sitting in the forecourt of her noodle shop. Several tables were occupied by office-workers having their lunch.

"Poor Kazuo-San," I said, with a laugh. "But I can understand how he feels. It was so sad about Miss Michiko. And they were engaged for a long time, weren't they?"

"Three years. I never saw the point in these long engagements. Yes, Michiko was a nice girl. I'm sure she'd be the first to agree with me about Kazuo mourning her like this. She would have wanted him to continue with his life."

"It must be difficult for him though. To have built up plans for so long only for things to end like that."

"But that's all in the past now," said Mrs Fujiwara. "We've all had to put things behind us. You too, Etsuko, I remember you were very heartbroken once. But you managed to carry on."

"Yes, but I was fortunate. Ogata-San was very kind to me in those days. I don't know what would have become of me otherwise."

"Yes, he was very kind to you. And of course, that's how you met your husband. But you deserved to be fortunate."

"I really don't know where I'd be today if Ogata-San hadn't taken me in. But I can understand how difficult it must be — for your son, I mean. Even me I still think about Nakamura-San sometimes. I can't help it. Sometimes I wake up and forget. I think I'm still back here, here in Nakagawa . . ."

"Now, Etsuko, that's no way to talk." Mrs Fujiwara looked at me for some moments, then gave a sigh. "But it happens to me too. Like you say, in the mornings, just as you wake, it can catch you unawares. I often wake up thinking I'll have to hurry and get breakfast ready for them all."

We fell silent for a moment. Then Mrs Fujiwara laughed a little.

"You're very bad, Etsuko," she said. "See, you've got me talking like this now."

"It's very foolish of me," I said. "In any case, Nakamura-San and I, there was never anything between us. I mean, nothing had been decided."

Mrs Fujiwara went on looking at me, nodding to some private train of thought. Then across the forecourt a customer stood up, ready to leave.

I watched Mrs Fujiwara go over to him, a neat young man in shirt-sleeves. They bowed to each other and began chatting cheerfully. The man made some remark as he buttoned his briefcase and Mrs Fujiwara laughed heartily. They exchanged bows once more, then he disappeared into the afternoon rush. I was grateful for the opportunity to compose my emotions. When Mrs Fujiwara came back, I said:

"I'd better be leaving you soon. You're very busy just now."

"You just stay there and relax. You've only just sat down. I'll get you some lunch."

"No, that's all right."

"Now, Etsuko, if you don't eat here, you won't eat lunch for another hour. You know how important it is for you to eat regularly at this stage."

"Yes, I suppose so."

Mrs Fujiwara looked at me closely for a moment. Then she said: "You've everything to look forward to now, Etsuko. What are you so unhappy about?"

"Unhappy? But I'm not unhappy in the least."

She continued to look at me, and I laughed nervously.

"Once the child comes," she said, "you'll be delighted, believe me. And you'll make a splendid mother, Etsuko."

"I hope so."

"Of course you will."

"Yes." I looked up and smiled.

Mrs Fujiwara nodded, then rose to her feet once more.

The inside of Sachiko's cottage had grown increasingly dark — there was only one lantern in the room — and at first I thought Mariko was staring at a black mark on the wall. She reached out a finger and the shape moved a little. Only then did I realize it was a spider.

"Mariko, leave that alone. That's not nice."

She put both hands behind her back, but went on staring at the spider.

"We used to have a cat once," she said. "Before we came here. She used to catch spiders."

"I see. No, leave it alone, Mariko."

"But it's not poisonous."

"No, but leave it alone, it's dirty."

"The cat we used to have, she could eat spiders. What would happen if I ate a spider?"

"I don't know, Mariko."

"Would I be sick?"

"I don't know." I went back to the sewing I had brought with me. Mariko continued to watch the spider. Eventually she said: "I know why you came here tonight."

"I came because it's not nice for little girls to be on their own."

"It's because of the woman. It's because the woman might come again."

"Why don't you show me some more drawings? The ones you showed me just now were lovely."

Mariko did not reply. She moved over to the window and looked out into the darkness.

"Your mother won't be long now," I said. "Why don't you show me some more drawings."

78

Mariko continued to look into the darkness. Eventually, she returned to the corner where she had been sitting before the spider had attracted her attention.

"How did you spend your day today, Mariko?" I asked. "Did you do any drawing?"

"I played with Atsu and Mee-Chan."

"That's nice. And where do they live? Are they from the apartments?"

"That's Atsu" — she pointed to one of the small black kittens beside her — "and that's Mee-Chan."

I laughed. "Oh, I see. They're lovely little kittens, aren't they? But don't you ever play with other children? The children from the apartments?"

"I play with Atsu and Mee-Chan."

"But you should try and make friends with the other children. I'm sure they're all very nice."

"They stole Suji-Chan. He was my favourite kitten."

"They stole him? Oh dear, I wonder why they did that."

Mariko began stroking a kitten. "I've lost Suji-Chan now."

"Perhaps he'll turn up soon. I'm sure the children were just playing."

"They killed him. I've lost Suji-Chan now."

"Oh. I wonder why they did a thing like that."

"I threw stones at them. Because they said things."

"Well, you shouldn't throw stones, Mariko."

"They said things. About Mother. I threw stones at them and they took Suji-Chan and wouldn't give him back."

"Well, you've still got your other kittens."

Mariko moved across the room towards the window again. She was just tall enough to lean her elbows on the ledge. For a few minutes she looked into the darkness, her face close to the pane.

"I want to go out now," she said, suddenly.

"Go out? But it's far too late, it's dark outside. And your mother will be back any time now."

79

"But I want to go out."

"Stay here now, Mariko."

She continued to look outside. I tried to see what was visible to her; from where I sat I could see only darkness.

"Perhaps you should be kinder to the other children. Then you could make friends with them."

"I know why Mother asked you to come here."

"You can't expect to make friends if you throw stones."

"It's because of the woman. It's because Mother knows about the woman."

"I don't understand what you're talking about, Mariko-San. Tell me more about your kittens. Will you draw more pictures of them when they get bigger?"

"It's because the woman might come again. That's why Mother asked you."

"I don't think so."

"Mother's seen the woman. She saw her the other night."

I stopped sewing for a second and looked up at Mariko. She had turned away from the window and was gazing at me with a strangely expressionless look.

"Where did your mother see this — this person?"

"Out there. She saw her out there. That's why she asked you."

Mariko came away from the window and returned to her kittens. The older cat had appeared and the kittens had curled up to their mother. Mariko lay down beside them and started to whisper. Her whispering had a vaguely disturbing quality.

"Your mother should be home soon," I said. "I wonder what she can be doing."

Mariko continued whispering.

"She was telling me all about Frank-San," I said. "He sounds a very nice man."

The whispering noises stopped. We stared at each other for a second.

"He's a bad man," Mariko said.

"Now that's not a nice thing to say, Mariko-San. Your mother told me all about him and he sounds very nice. And I'm sure he's very kind to you, isn't he?"

She got to her feet and went to the wall. The spider was still there.

"Yes, I'm sure he's a nice man. He's kind to you, isn't he, Mariko-San?"

Mariko reached forward. The spider moved quite slowly along the wall.

"Mariko, leave that alone."

"The cat we had in Tokyo, she used to catch spiders. We were going to bring her with us."

I could see the spider more clearly in its new position. It had thick short legs, each leg casting a shadow on the yellow wall.

"She was a good cat," Mariko continued. "She was going to come with us to Nagasaki."

"And did you bring her?"

"She disappeared. The day before we were leaving. Mother promised we could bring her, but she disappeared."

"I see."

She moved suddenly and caught one of the spider's legs. The remaining legs crawled frantically around her hand as she brought it away from the wall.

"Mariko, let that go. That's dirty."

Mariko turned over her hand and the spider crawled into her palm. She closed her other hand over it so that it was imprisoned.

"Mariko, put that down."

"It's not poisonous," she said, coming closer to me.

"No, but it's dirty. Put it back in the corner."

"It's not poisonous though."

She stood in front of me, the spider inside her cupped hands. Through a gap in her fingers, I could see a leg moving slowly and rhythmically.

"Put it back in the corner, Mariko."

"What would happen if I ate it? It's not poisonous."

"You'd be very sick. Now, Mariko, put it back in the corner."

Mariko brought the spider closer to her face and parted her lips.

"Don't be silly, Mariko. That's very dirty."

Her mouth opened wider, and then her hands parted and the spider landed in front of my lap. I started back. The spider sped along the tatami into the shadows behind me. It took me a moment to recover, and by then Mariko had left the cottage.

Chapter Six

I cannot be sure now how long I spent searching for her that night. Quite possibly it was for a considerable time, for I was advanced in my pregnancy by then and careful to avoid hurried movements. Besides, once having come outside, I was finding it strangely peaceful to walk beside the river. Along one section of the bank, the grass had grown very tall. I must have been wearing sandals that night for I can remember distinctly the feel of the grass on my feet. As I walked, there were insects making noises all around me.

Then eventually I became aware of a separate sound, a rustling noise as if a snake were sliding in the grass behind me. I stopped to listen, then realized what had caused it; an old piece of rope had tangled itself around my ankle and I had been dragging it through the grass. I carefully released it from around my foot. When I held it up to the moonlight it felt damp and muddy between my fingers.

"Hello, Mariko," I said, for she was sitting in the grass a short way in front of me, her knees hunched up to her chin. A willow tree — one of several that grew on the bank — hung over the spot where she sat. I took a few steps towards her until I could make out her face more clearly.

"What's that?" she asked.

"Nothing. It just tangled on to my foot when I was walking."

"What is it though?"

"Nothing, just a piece of old rope. Why are you out here?"

"Do you want to take a kitten?"

"A kitten?"

"Mother says we can't keep the kittens. Do you want one?"

"I don't think so."

"But we have to find homes for them soon. Or else Mother says we'll have to drown them."

"That would be a pity."

"You could have Atsu."

"We'll have to see."

"Why have you got that?"

"I told you, it's nothing. It just caught on to my foot." I took a step closer. "Why are you doing that, Mariko?"

"Doing what?"

"You were making a strange face just now."

"I wasn't making a strange face. Why have you got the rope?"

"You were making a strange face. It was a very strange face."

"Why have you got the rope?"

I watched her for a moment. Signs of fear were appearing on her face.

"Don't you want a kitten then?" she asked.

"No, I don't think so. What's the matter with you?"

Mariko got to her feet. I came forward until I reached the willow tree. I noticed the cottage a short distance away, the shape of its roof darker than the sky. I could hear Mariko's footsteps running off into the darkness.

When I reached the door of the cottage, I could hear Sachiko's voice from within, talking angrily. They both turned to me as I came in. Sachiko was standing in the middle of the room, her daughter before her. In the light cast by the lantern, her carefully prepared face had a mask-like quality.

"I fear Mariko's been giving you trouble," she said to me.

"Well, she ran outside . . ."

"Say sorry to Etsuko-San." She gripped Mariko's arm roughly.

"I want to go outside again."

"You won't move. Now apologize."

"I want to go outside."

With her free hand, Sachiko slapped the child sharply on the back of her thigh. "Now, apologize to Etsuko-San."

Small tears were appearing in Mariko's eyes. She looked at me briefly, then turned back to her mother. "Why do you always go away?"

Sachiko raised her hand again warningly.

"Why do you always go away with Frank-San?"

"Are you going to say you're sorry?"

"Frank-San pisses like a pig. He's a pig in a sewer."

Sachiko stared at her child, her hand still poised in the air.

"He drinks his own piss."

"Silence."

"He drinks his own piss and he shits in his bed."

Sachiko continued to glare, but remained quite still.

"He drinks his own piss." Mariko pulled her arm free and walked across the room with an air of nonchalance. At the entryway she turned and stared back at her mother. "He pisses like a pig," she repeated, then went out into the darkness.

Sachiko stared at the entryway for some moments, apparently oblivious of my presence.

"Shouldn't someone go after her?" I said, after a while.

Sachiko looked at me and seemed to relax a little. "No," she said, sitting down. "Leave her."

"But it's very late."

"Leave her. She can come back when she pleases."

A kettle had been steaming on the open stove for some time. Sachiko took it off the flame and began making tea. I watched her for several moments, then asked quietly:

85

"Did you find your friend?"

"Yes, Etsuko," she said. "I found him." She continued with her tea-making, not looking up at me. Then she said: "It was very kind of you to have come here tonight. I do apologize about Mariko."

I continued to watch her. Eventually, I said: "What are your plans now?"

"My plans?" Sachiko finished filling the teapot, then poured the remaining water on to the flame. "Etsuko, I've told you many times, what is of the utmost importance to me is my daughter's welfare. That must come before everything else. I'm a mother, after all. I'm not some young saloon girl with no regard for decency. I'm a mother, and my daughter's interests come first."

"Of course."

"I intend to write to my uncle. I'll inform him of my whereabouts and I'll tell him as much as he has a right to know about my present circumstances. Then if he wishes, I'll discuss with him the possibilities of our returning to his house." Sachiko picked up the teapot in both hands and began to shake it gently. "As a matter of fact, Etsuko, I'm rather glad things have turned out like this. Imagine how unsettling it would have been for my daughter, finding herself in a land full of foreigners, a land full of Ame-kos. And suddenly having an Ame-ko for a father, imagine how confusing that would be for her. Do you understand what I'm saying, Etsuko? She's had enough disturbance in her life already, she deserves to be somewhere settled. It's just as well things have turned out this way."

I murmured something in assent.

"Children, Etsuko," she went on, "mean responsibility. You'll discover that yourself soon enough. And that's what he's really scared of, anyone can see that. He's scared of Mariko. Well, that's not acceptable to me, Etsuko. My daughter comes first. It's just as well things have turned out this way." She went on rocking the teapot in her hands.

"This must be very distressing for you," I said, eventually.

"Distressing?" — Sachiko laughed — "Etsuko, do you imagine little things like this distress me? When I was your age, perhaps. But not any more. I've gone through too much over the last few years. In any case, I was expecting this to happen. Oh yes, I'm not surprised at all. I expected this. The last time, in Tokyo, it was much the same. He disappeared and spent all our money, drank it all in three days. A lot of it was my money too. Do you know, Etsuko, I actually worked as a maid in a hotel? Yes, as a maid. But I didn't complain, and we almost had enough, a few more weeks and we could have got a ship to America. But then he drank it all. All those weeks I spent scrubbing floors on my knees and he drank it all up in three days. And now there he is again, in a bar with his worthless saloon girl. How can I place my daughter's future in the hands of a man like that? I'm a mother, and my daughter comes first."

We fell silent again. Sachiko put the teapot down in front of her and stared at it.

"I hope your uncle will prove understanding," I said.

She gave a shrug. "As far as my uncle's concerned, Etsuko, I'll discuss the matter with him. I'm willing to do so for Mariko's sake. If he proves unhelpful, then I'll just find some alternative course. In any case, I've no intention of accompanying some foreign drunkard to America. I'm quite happy he's found some saloon girl to drink with him, I'm sure they deserve one another. But as far as I'm concerned, I'm going to do what's best for Mariko, and that's my decision."

For some time, Sachiko continued to stare at the teapot. Then she sighed and got to her feet. She went over to the window and peered out into the darkness.

"Should we go and look for her now?" I said.

"No," Sachiko said, still looking out. "She'll be back soon. Let her stay out if that's what she wants."

I feel only regret now for those attitudes I displayed towards Keiko. In this country, after all, it is not unexpected that a young woman of that age should wish to leave home. All I succeeded in doing, it would seem, was to ensure that when she finally left — now almost six years ago — she did so severing all her ties with me. But then I never imagined she could so quickly vanish beyond my reach; all I saw was that my daughter, unhappy as she was at home, would find the world outside too much for her. It was for her own protection I opposed her so vehemently.

That morning — the fifth day of Niki's visit — I awoke during the early hours. What occurred to me first was that I could no longer hear the rain as on previous nights and mornings. Then I remembered what had awoken me.

I lay under the covers looking in turn at those objects visible in the pale light. After several minutes, I felt somewhat calmer and closed my eyes again. I did not sleep, however. I thought of the landlady — Keiko's landlady — and how she had finally opened the door of that room in Manchester.

I opened my eyes and once more looked at the objects in the room. Finally I rose and put on my dressing gown. I made my way to the bathroom, taking care not to arouse Niki, asleep in the spare room next to mine. When I came out of the bathroom, I remained standing on the landing for some time. Beyond the staircase, at the far end of the hallway, I could see the door of Keiko's room. The door, as usual, was shut. I went on staring at it, then moved a few steps forward. Eventually, I found myself standing before it. Once, as I stood there, I thought I heard a small sound, some movement from within. I listened for a while but the sound did not come again. I reached forward and opened the door.

Keiko's room looked stark in the greyish light; a bed covered with a single sheet, her white dressing table, and on the floor, several cardboard boxes containing those of her belongings she had not taken with her to Manchester. I stepped further into the room. The curtains had been left open and I could see the orchard below. The sky looked pale and white; it did not appear to be raining. Beneath the window, down on the grass, two birds were pecking at some fallen apples. I started to feel the cold then and returned to my room.

"A friend of mine's writing a poem about you," said Niki. We were eating breakfast in the kitchen.

"About me? Why on earth is she doing that?"

"I was telling her about you and she decided she'd write a poem. She's a brilliant poet."

"A poem about me? How absurd. What is there to write about? She doesn't even know me."

"I just said, Mother. I told her about you. It's amazing how well she understands people. She's been through quite a bit herself, you see."

"I see. And how old is this friend of yours?"

"Mother, you're always so obsessed about how old people are. It doesn't matter how old someone is, it's what they've experienced that counts. People can get to be a hundred and not experience a thing."

"I suppose so." I gave a laugh and glanced towards the windows. Outside, it had started to drizzle.

"I was telling her about you," Niki said. "About you and Dad and how you left Japan. She was really impressed. She appreciates what it must have been like, how it wasn't quite as easy as it sounds."

For a moment, I went on gazing at the windows. Then I said quickly: "I'm sure your friend will write a marvellous poem." I took an apple from the fruit basket and Niki watched as I began to peel it with my knife.

"So many women", she said, "get stuck with kids and

89

lousy husbands and they're just miserable. But they can't pluck up the courage to do a thing about it. They'll just go on like that for the rest of their lives."

"I see. So you're saying they should desert their children, are you, Niki?"

"You know what I mean. It's pathetic when people just waste away their lives."

I did not speak, although my daughter paused as if expecting me to do so.

"It couldn't have been easy, what you did, Mother. You ought to be proud of what you did with your life."

I continued to peel the apple. When I had finished, I dried my fingers on the napkin.

"My friends all think so too," said Niki. "The ones I've told anyway."

"I'm very flattered. Please thank your marvellous friends."

"I was just saying, that's all."

"Well, you've made your point quite clearly now."

Perhaps I was unnecessarily curt with her that morning, but then it was presumptious of Niki to suppose I would need reassuring on such matters. Besides, she has little idea of what actually occurred during those last days in Nagasaki. One supposes she has built up some sort of picture from what her father has told her. Such a picture, inevitably, would have its inaccuracies. For, in truth, despite all the impressive articles he wrote about Japan, my husband never understood the ways of our culture, even less a man like Jiro. I do not claim to recall Jiro with affection, but then he was never the oafish man my husband considered him to be. Jiro worked hard to do his part for the family and he expected me to do mine; in his own terms, he was a dutiful husband. And indeed, for the seven years he knew his daughter, he was a good father to her. Whatever else I convinced myself of during those final days, I never pretended Keiko would not miss him.

But such things are long in the past now and I have no wish to ponder them yet again. My motives for leaving Japan were justifiable, and I know I always kept Keiko's interests very much at heart. There is nothing to be gained in going over such matters again.

I had been pruning the pot plants along the window ledge for some time when I realized how quiet Niki had become. When I turned to her, she was standing in front of the fireplace, looking past me out into the garden. I turned back to the window, trying to follow her gaze; despite the mist on the pane, the garden was still clearly discernible. Niki, it seemed, was gazing over to a spot near the hedge, where the rain and wind had put into disarray the canes which supported the young tomato plants.

"I think the tomatoes are ruined for this year," I said. "I've really rather neglected them."

I was still looking at the canes when I heard the sound of a drawer being pulled open, and when I turned again, Niki was continuing with her search. She had decided after breakfast to read through all her father's newspaper articles, and had spent much of the morning going through all the drawers and bookshelves in the house.

For some minutes, I continued working on my pot plants; there were a large number of them, cluttering the window ledge. Behind me, I could hear Niki going through the drawers. Then she became quiet again, and when I turned to her, she was once more gazing past me, out into the garden.

"I think I'll go and do the goldfish now," she said.

"The goldfish?"

Without replying, Niki left the room, and a moment later I saw her go striding across the lawn. I wiped away a little mist from the pane and watched her. Niki walked to the far end of the garden, to the fish-pond amidst the rockery. She

91

poured in the feed, and for several seconds remained standing there, gazing into the pond. I could see her figure in profile; she looked very thin, and despite her fashionable clothes there was still something unmistakably childlike about her. I watched the wind disturb her hair and wondered why she had gone outside without a jacket.

On her way back, she stopped beside the tomato plants and in spite of the heavy drizzle stood contemplating them for some time. Then she took a few steps closer and with much care began straightening the canes. She stood up several that had fallen completely, then, crouching down so her knees almost touched the wet grass, adjusted the net I had laid above the soil to protect the plants from marauding birds.

"Thank you, Niki," I said to her when she came in. "That was very thoughtful of you."

She muttered something and sat down on the settee. I noticed she had become quite embarrassed.

"I really have been rather neglectful about those tomatoes this year," I went on. "Still, it doesn't really matter, I suppose. I never know what to do with so many tomatoes these days. Last year, I gave most of them to the Morrisons."

"Oh God," said Niki, "the Morrisons. And how are the dear old Morrisons?"

"Niki, the Morrisons are perfectly kind people. I've never understood why you need to be so disparaging. You and Cathy used to be the best of friends once."

"Oh yes, Cathy. And how's she these days? Still living at home, I suppose?"

"Well, yes. She works in a bank now."

"Typical enough."

"That seems to me a perfectly sensible thing to be doing at her age. And Marilyn's married now, did you know?"

"Oh yes? And who did she marry?"

"I don't remember what her husband does. I met him

once. He seemed very pleasant."

"I expect he's a vicar or something like that."

"Now, Niki, I really don't see why you have to adopt this tone. The Morrisons have always been extremely kind to us."

Niki sighed impatiently. "It's just the way they do things," she said. "It makes me sick. Like the way they've brought up their kids."

"But you've hardly seen the Morrisons in years."

"I saw them often enough when I used to know Cathy. People like that are so hopeless. I suppose I ought to feel sorry for Cathy."

"You're blaming her because she hasn't gone to live in London like you have? I must say, Niki, that doesn't sound like the broadmindedness you and your friends seem so proud of."

"Oh, it doesn't matter. You don't understand what I'm talking about anyway." She glanced towards me, then heaved another sigh. "It doesn't matter," she repeated, looking the other way.

I continued to stare at her for a moment. Eventually, I turned back to the window ledge and for some minutes worked on in silence.

"You know, Niki," I said, after some time, "I'm very pleased you have good friends you enjoy being with. After all, you must lead your own life now. That's only to be expected."

My daughter gave no reply. When I glanced at her, she was reading one of the newspapers she had found in the drawer.

"I'd be interested to meet your friends," I said. "You're always welcome to bring any of them here."

Niki flicked her head to prevent her hair falling across her vision, and continued to read. A look of concentration had appeared on her face.

I went back to my plants, for I could read these signals

well enough. There is a certain subtle and yet quiet emphatic manner Niki adopts whenever I display curiosity concerning her life in London; it is her way of telling me I will regret it if I persist. Consequently, my picture of her present life is built largely upon speculation. In her letters, however — and Niki is very good about remembering to write — she mentions certain things she would never touch upon in conversation. That is how I have learnt, for instance, that her boyfriend's name is David and that he is studying politics at one of the London colleges. And yet, during conversation, if I were even to enquire after his health, I know that barrier would come firmly down.

This rather aggressive regard for privacy reminds me very much of her sister. For in truth, my two daughters had much in common, much more than my husband would ever admit. As far as he was concerned, they were complete opposites; furthermore, it became his view that Keiko was a difficult person by nature and there was little we could do for her. In fact, although he never claimed it outright, he would imply that Keiko had inherited her personality from her father. I did little to contradict this, for it was the easy explanation, that Jiro was to blame, not us. Of course, my husband never knew Keiko in her early years; if he had, he may well have recognized how similar the two girls were during their respective early stages. Both had fierce tempers, both were possessive; if they became upset, they would not like other children forget their anger quickly, but would remain moody for most of the day. And yet, one has become a happy, confident young woman — I have every hope for Niki's future — while the other, after becoming increasingly miserable, took her own life. I do not find it as easy as my husband did to put the blame on Nature, or else on Jiro. However, such things are in the past now, and there is little to be gained in going over them here.

"By the way, Mother," said Niki. "That *was* you this

94

morning, wasn't it?"

"This morning?"

"I heard these sounds this morning. Really early, about four o'clock."

"I'm sorry I disturbed you. Yes, that was me." I began to laugh. "Why, who else did you imagine it was?" I continued to laugh, and for a moment could not stop. Niki stared at me, her newspaper still held open before her. "Well, I'm sorry I woke you, Niki," I said, finally controlling my laughter.

"It's all right, I was awake anyway. I can't seem to sleep properly these days."

"And after all that fuss you made about the rooms. Perhaps you should see a doctor."

"Maybe I will." Niki went back to her newspaper.

I laid down the clippers I had been using and turned to her. "You know, it's strange. I had that dream again this morning."

"What dream?"

"I was telling you about it yesterday, but I don't suppose you were listening. I dreamt about that little girl again."

"What little girl?"

"The one we saw playing on the swing the other day. When we were in the village having coffee."

Niki shrugged. "Oh, that one," she said, not looking up.

"Well, actually, it isn't that little girl at all. That's what I realized this morning. It seemed to be that little girl, but it wasn't."

Niki looked at me again. Then she said: "I suppose you mean it was her. Keiko."

"Keiko?" I laughed a little. "What a strange idea. Why should it be Keiko? No, it was nothing to do with Keiko."

Niki continued to look at me uncertainly.

"It was just a little girl I knew once," I said to her. "A long time ago."

"Which little girl?"

"No one you know. I knew her a long time ago."

Niki gave another shrug. "I can't even get to sleep in the first place. I think I only slept about four hours last night."

"That's rather disturbing, Niki. Especially at your age. Perhaps you should see a doctor. You can always go and see Dr Ferguson."

Niki made another of her impatient gestures and went back to her father's newspaper article. I watched her for a moment.

"In fact, I realized something else this morning," I said. "Something else about the dream."

My daughter did not seem to hear.

"You see," I said, "the little girl isn't on a swing at all. It seemed like that at first. But it's not a swing she's on."

Niki murmured something and carried on reading.

PART TWO

Chapter Seven

As the summer grew hotter, the stretch of wasteground outside our apartment block became increasingly unpleasant. Much of the earth lay dried and cracked, while water which had accumulated during the rainy season remained in the deeper ditches and craters. The ground bred all manner of insects, and the mosquitoes in particular seemed everywhere. In the apartments there was the usual complaining, but over the years the anger over the wasteground had become resigned and cynical.

I crossed that ground regularly that summer to reach Sachiko's cottage, and indeed it was a loathsome journey; insects often caught in one's hair, and there were grubs and midges visible amidst the cracked surface. I still remember those journeys vividly, and they — like those misgivings about motherhood, like Ogata-San's visit — serve today to bring a certain distinctness to that summer. And yet in many ways, that summer was much like any other. I spent many moments — as I was to do throughout succeeding years — gazing emptily at the view from my apartment window. On clearer days, I could see far beyond the trees on the opposite bank of the river, a pale outline of hills visible against the clouds. It was not an unpleasant view, and on occasions it brought me a rare sense of relief from the emptiness of those long afternoons I spent in that apartment.

Apart from the matter of the wasteground, there were other topics which preoccupied the neighbourhood that summer. The newspapers were full of talk about the occupation coming to an end and in Tokyo politicians were

99

busy in argument with each other. In the apartments, the issue was discussed frequently enough, but with much the same cynicism as coloured talk concerning the waste-ground. Received with more urgency were the reports of the child murders that were alarming Nagasaki at the time. First a boy, then a small girl had been found battered to death. When a third victim, another little girl, had been found hanging from a tree there was near-panic amongst the mothers in the neighbourhood. Understandably, little comfort was taken from the fact that the incidents had taken place on the other side of the city: children became a rare sight around the housing precinct, particularly in the evening hours.

I am not sure to what extent these reports worried Sachiko at the time. Certainly she seemed less inclined to leave Mariko unattended, but then I suspect this had more to do with other developments in her life; she had received a reply from her uncle, expressing his willingness to take her back into his household, and soon after this news, I noticed a change come over Sachiko's attitude to the little girl: she seemed somehow more patient and relaxed with the child.

Sachiko had betrayed much relief about her uncle's letter, and at first I had little reason to doubt she would return to his house. However, as the days went by, my suspicions grew about her intentions. For one thing, I discovered some days after the arrival of the letter that Sachiko had not yet mentioned the matter to Mariko. And then, as the weeks went on, not only did Sachiko make no preparations for moving, she had not, so I discovered, sent a reply to her uncle.

Had Sachiko not been so peculiarly reluctant to talk about her uncle's household, I doubt if it would have occurred to me to ponder such a topic. As it was, I grew curious, and despite Sachiko's reticence I managed to gather certain impressions; for one thing, the uncle was not, it seemed,

100

related by blood, but was a relative of Sachiko's husband; Sachiko had never known him prior to arriving at his house several months earlier. The uncle was wealthy, and since his house was an unusually large one — and his daughter and a housemaid the only other occupants — there had been plenty of room for Sachiko and her little girl. Indeed, one thing Sachiko did mention more than once was her recollection of how large parts of that house had remained empty and silent.

In particular, I became curious about the uncle's daughter, who I gathered to be an unmarried woman of roughly Sachiko's age. Sachiko would say little about her cousin, but then I do recall one conversation we had around that time. I had by then formed an idea that Sachiko's slowness in returning to her uncle had to do with some tension which existed between herself and the cousin. I must have tentatively put this to Sachiko that morning, for it provoked one of the few occasions upon which she talked explicitly about the time she had spent at her uncle's house. The conversation comes back to me quite vividly; it was one of those dry windless mornings of mid-August, and we were standing on the bridge at the top of our hill, waiting for a tram to take us into the city. I cannot remember where it was we were going that day, or where we had left Mariko — for I recall the child was not with us. Sachiko was gazing out at the view from the bridge, holding up a hand to shield her face from the sun.

"It puzzles me, Etsuko," she said, "how you ever managed to get hold of such an idea. On the contrary, Yasuko and I were the best of friends, and I'm greatly looking forward to seeing her again. I really don't understand how you could have thought otherwise, Etsuko."

"I'm sorry, I must have been mistaken," I said. "For some reason, I supposed you had some reservations about returning there."

"Not at all, Etsuko. When you first met me, it's quite

true, I was in the process of considering certain other possibilities. But a mother can't be blamed for considering the different options that arise for her child, can she? It just so happened that for a while there seemed an interesting option open to us. But having given it further consideration, I've now rejected it. That's all there is to it, Etsuko, I've no further interest in these other plans that were suggested to me. I'm glad everything has turned out for the best, and I'm looking forward to returning to my uncle's house. As for Yasuko-San, we have the highest regard for each other. I don't understand what could have made you suppose otherwise, Etsuko."

"I do apologize. It's just that I thought you once mentioned a quarrel of some kind."

"A quarrel?" She looked at me for a second, and then a smile spread over her face. "Oh, now I understand what you're referring to. No, Etsuko, that was no quarrel. That was just some trivial tiff we had. What was it about now? You see, I don't even remember, it was so trivial. Oh yes, that's right, we were arguing about which of us should prepare the supper. Yes, really, that's all it was. You see, Etsuko, we used to take it in turns. The housemaid would cook one night, my cousin the next, then it would be my turn. The housemaid was taken ill on one of her nights, and Yasuko and I both wanted to cook. Now you mustn't misunderstand, Etsuko, we generally got on very well. It's just that when you see so much of one person and no one else, things can get out of proportion at times."

"Yes, I do understand. I'm sorry, I was quite mistaken."

"You see, Etsuko, when you have a housemaid to do all the little jobs for you, it's surprising how slowly the time goes by. Yasuko and I, we tried to occupy ourselves one way or another, but really there was little to do other than sit and talk all day. All those months we sat in that house together, we hardly saw an outsider the whole time. It's a wonder we didn't really quarrel. Properly, I mean."

"Yes, it certainly is. I obviously misunderstood you before."

"Yes, Etsuko, I'm afraid you did. I only happen to remember the incident because it occurred just before we left and I haven't seen my cousin since. But it's absurd to call it a quarrel." She gave a laugh. "In fact, I expect Yasuko's thinking of it and laughing too."

Perhaps it was that same morning, we decided that before Sachiko went away, we would go together on a day's outing somewhere. And indeed, one hot afternoon not long afterwards, I accompanied Sachiko and her daughter to Inasa. Inasa is the hilly area of Nagasaki overlooking the harbour, renowned for its mountain scenery; it was not so far from where we lived — in fact it was the hills of Inasa I could see from my apartment window — but in those days, outings of any sort were rare for me, and the trip to Inasa seemed like a major excursion. I remember I looked forward to it for days; it is, I suppose, one of the better memories I have from those times.

We crossed to Inasa by ferry at the height of the afternoon. Noises from the harbour followed us across the water — the clang of hammers, the whine of machinery, the occasional deep sound from a ship's horn — but in those days, in Nagasaki, such sounds were not unpleasing; they were the sounds of recovery and they were still capable then of bringing a certain uplifting feeling to one's spirits.

Once we had crossed the water, the sea-winds seemed to blow more freely and the day no longer felt so stifling. The sounds of the harbour, carried in the wind, still reached us as we sat on a bench in the forecourt of the cable-car station. We were all the more grateful for the breeze, for the forecourt offered scant shelter from the sun; it was simply an open area of concrete which — being peopled that day largely by children and their mothers — resembled a

103

school playground. Over to one side, behind a set of turnstiles, we could see the wooden platforms where the cable-cars came to rest. For some moments we sat mesmerized by the sight of the cable-cars climbing and falling; one car would go rising away into the trees, gradually turning into a small dot against the sky, while its companion came lower, growing larger, until it heaved itself to a halt at the platform. Inside a small hut beside the turnstiles, a man was operating some levers; he wore a cap, and after each car had come down safely, he would lean out and chat to a group of children who had gathered to watch.

The first of our encounters that day with the American woman occurred as a result of our deciding to take the cable-car to the hilltop. Sachiko and her daughter had gone to buy the tickets and for a moment I was left sitting alone on the bench. Then I noticed at the far end of the forecourt a small stall selling sweets and toys. Thinking I would perhaps buy some candy for Mariko, I got to my feet and walked over to it. Two children were there before me, arguing about what to buy. While I waited for them, I noticed among the toys a pair of plastic binoculars. The children continued to quarrel, and I glanced back across the forecourt. Sachiko and Mariko were still standing by the turnstiles; Sachiko seemed to be in conversation with two women.

"Can I be of service, madam?"

The children had gone. Behind the stall was a young man in a neat summer uniform.

"May I try these?" I pointed to the binoculars.

"Certainly, madam. It's just a toy, but quite effective."

I put the binoculars to my face and looked towards the hill-slope; they were surprisingly powerful. I turned to the forecourt and found Sachiko and her daughter in the lenses. Sachiko had dressed for the day in a light-coloured kimono tied with an elegant sash — a costume, I suspected, reserved only for special occasions — and she cut a

104

graceful figure amidst the crowd. She was still talking to the two women, one of whom looked like a foreigner.

"A hot day again, madam," the young man said, as I handed him the money. "Are you riding on the cable-car?"

"We're just about to."

"It's a magnificent view. That's a television tower we're building on the top. By next year, the cable-car will go right up to it, right to the top."

"How splendid. Have a nice day, won't you."

"Thank you, madam."

I made my way back across the forecourt with the binoculars. Although at that time I did not understand English, I guessed at once that the foreign woman was American. She was tall, with red wavy hair and glasses which pointed up at the corners. She was addressing Sachiko in a loud voice, and I noted with surprise the ease with which Sachiko replied in English. The other woman was Japanese; she had noticeably plump features, and appeared to be around forty or so. Beside her was a tubby little boy of about eight or nine. I bowed to them as I arrived, wished them a pleasant day, then handed Mariko the binoculars.

"It's just a toy," I said. "But you might be able to see a few things."

Mariko opened the wrapping and examined the binoculars with a serious expression. She looked through them, first around the forecourt, then up at the hill-slope.

"Say thank you, Mariko," Sachiko said.

Mariko continued to look through the binoculars. Then she brought them away from her face and put the plastic strap over her head.

"Thank you, Etsuko-San," she said, a little grudgingly.

The American woman pointed to the binoculars, said something in English and laughed. The binoculars had also attracted the attention of the tubby boy, who previously had been watching the hill-slope and the descending cable-car. He took a few steps towards Mariko, his eyes on the binoculars.

"That was very kind of you, Etsuko," said Sachiko.

"Not at all. It's just a toy."

The cable-car arrived and we went through the turnstiles, on to the hollow wooden boards. The two women and the tubby boy, it seemed, were to be the only other passengers. The man with the cap came out of his hut and ushered us one by one into the car. The interior looked stark and metallic. There were large windows on all sides and benches ran along the two larger walls.

The car remained at the platform for several more minutes and the tubby boy began to walk around impatiently. Beside me, Mariko was looking out of the window, her knees up on the bench. From our side of the car, we could see the forecourt and the gathering of young spectators at the turnstiles. Mariko seemed to be testing the effectiveness of her binoculars, holding them to her eyes one moment, taking them away the next. Then the tubby boy came and knelt on the bench beside her. For a little while, the two children ignored each other. Finally, the boy said:

"I want to have a look now." He held out his hand for the binoculars. Mariko looked at him coldly.

"Akira, don't ask like that," said his mother. "Ask the little lady nicely."

The boy took his hand away and looked at Mariko. The little girl stared back. The boy turned and went to another window.

The children at the turnstiles waved as the car began to pull away. I instinctively reached for the metal bar running along the window, and the American woman made a nervous noise and laughed. The forecourt was growing smaller and then the hillside began to move beneath us; the cable-car swayed gently as we climbed higher; for a moment, the treetops seemed to brush against the

106

windows, then suddenly a large dip opened beneath us and we were hanging in the sky. Sachiko laughed softly and pointed to something out of the window. Mariko continued to look through her binoculars.

The cable-car finished its climb and we filed out cautiously as if uncertain we had arrived on solid ground. The higher station had no concrete forecourt, and we stepped off the wooden boards into a small grass clearing. Other than the uniformed man who ushered us out, there were no other people in sight. At the back of the clearing, almost amidst the pine trees, stood several wooden picnic tables. The near edge of the clearing where we had disembarked was marked by a metal fence, which separated us from a cliff-edge. When we had regained our bearings a little, we wandered over to the fence and looked out over the falling mountainside. After a moment, the two women and the boy joined us.

"Quite breathtaking, isn't it?" the Japanese woman said to me. "I'm just showing my friend all the interesting sights. She's never been in Japan before."

"I see. I hope she's enjoying it here."

"I hope so. Unfortunately, I don't understand English so well. Your friend seems to speak it much better than I do."

"Yes, she speaks it very well."

We both glanced towards Sachiko. She and the American woman were again exchanging remarks in English.

"How nice to be so well educated," the woman said to me. "Well, I hope you all have a nice day."

We exchanged bows, then the woman made gestures to her American guest, suggesting they move off.

"Please may I look," the tubby boy said, in an angry voice. Again, he was holding out his hand. Mariko stared at him, as she had done in the cable-car.

"I want to see it," the boy said, more fiercely.

"Akira, remember to ask the little lady nicely."

"Please! I want to see it."

107

Mariko continued to look at him for a second, then took the plastic strap from around her neck and handed the boy the binoculars. The boy put them to his face and for some moments gazed over the fence.

"These aren't any good," he said finally, turning to his mother. "They aren't nearly as good as mine. Mother, look, you can't even see those trees over there properly. Take a look."

He held the binoculars towards his mother. Mariko reached for them but the boy snatched them away and again offered them to the woman.

"Take a look, Mother. You can't even see those trees, the near ones."

"Akira, give them back to the little lady now."

"They aren't nearly as good as mine."

"Now, Akira, that's not a nice thing to say. You know everyone isn't as lucky as you."

Mariko reached for the binoculars and this time the boy let go.

"Say thank you to the little lady," said his mother.

The boy said nothing and started to walk away. The mother laughed a little.

"Thank you very much," she said to Mariko. "You were very kind." Then she smiled in turn towards Sachiko and myself. "Splendid scenery, isn't it?" she said. "I do hope you have a nice day."

The path was covered with pine needles and rose up the side of the mountain in zig-zags. We walked at an easy pace, often stopping to rest. Mariko was quiet and — rather to my surprise — showed no signs of wishing to misbehave. She did however display a curious reluctance to walk alongside her mother and myself. One moment she would be lagging behind, causing us to cast anxious glances over our shoulders; the next moment, she would go running past us and walk on ahead.

We met the American woman for the second time an hour or so after we had disembarked from the cable-car. She and her companion were coming back down the path and, recognizing us, gave cheerful greetings. The tubby boy, coming behind them, ignored us. As she passed, the American woman said something to Sachiko in English, and when Sachiko replied, gave a loud laugh. She seemed to want to stop and talk, but the Japanese woman and her son did not break their step; the American woman waved and walked on.

When I complimented Sachiko on her command of English, she laughed and said nothing. The encounter, I noticed, had had a curious effect upon her. She became quiet, and walked on beside me as if lost in thought. Then, when Mariko had once more rushed on ahead, she said to me:

"My father was a highly respected man, Etsuko. Highly respected indeed. But his foreign connections almost resulted in my marriage proposal being withdrawn." She smiled slightly and shook her head. "How odd, Etsuko. That all seems like another age now."

"Yes," I said. "Things have changed so much."

The path bent sharply and began to climb again. The trees fell away and suddenly the sky seemed huge all around us. Up ahead, Mariko shouted something and pointed. Then she hurried on excitedly.

"I never saw a great deal of my father," Sachiko said. "He was abroad much of the time, in Europe and America. When I was young, I used to dream I'd go to America one day, that I'd go there and become a film actress. My mother used to laugh at me. But my father told me if I learnt my English well enough, I could easily become a business girl. I used to enjoy learning English."

Mariko had stopped at what looked like a plateau. She shouted something to us again.

109

"I remember once," Sachiko went on, "my father brought a book back from America for me, an English version of *A Christmas Carol*. That became something of an ambition of mine, Etsuko. I wanted to learn English well enough to read that book. Unfortunately, I never had the chance. When I married, my husband forbade me to continue learning. In fact, he made me throw the book away."

"That seems rather a pity," I said.

"My husband was like that, Etsuko. Very strict and very patriotic. He was never the most considerate of men. But he came from a highly distinguished family and my parents considered it a good match. I didn't protest when he forbade me to study English. After all, there seemed little point any more."

We reached the spot where Mariko was standing; it was a square area of ground that jutted off the edge of the path, bound in by several large boulders. A thick tree trunk fallen on to its side had been converted into a bench, the top surface having been smoothed and flattened. Sachiko and I sat down to recover our breath.

"Don't go too near the edge, Mariko," Sachiko called. The little girl had walked out to the boulders and was looking at the view with her binoculars.

I had a rather precarious feeling, perched on the edge of that mountain looking out over such a view; a long way down below us, we could see the harbour looking like a dense piece of machinery left in the water. Across the harbour, on the opposite bank, rose the series of hills that led into Nagasaki. The land at the foot of the hills was busy with houses and buildings. Far over to our right, the harbour opened out on to the sea.

We sat there for a while, recovering our breath and enjoying the breeze. Then I said:

"You wouldn't think anything had ever happened here, would you? Everything looks so full of life. But all that area down there" — I waved my hand at the view below us —

"all that area was so badly hit when the bomb fell. But look at it now."

Sachiko nodded, then turned to me with a smile. "How cheerful you are today, Etsuko," she said.

"But it's so good to come out here. Today I've decided I'm going to be optimistic. I'm determined to have a happy future. Mrs Fujiwara always tells me how important it is to keep looking forward. And she's right. If people didn't do that, then all this" — I pointed again at the view — "all this would still be rubble."

Sachiko smiled again. "Yes, as you say, Etsuko. It would all be rubble." For a few moments, she continued to gaze at the view below us. "Incidentally, Etsuko," she said, after a while, "your friend, Mrs Fujiwara. I assume she lost her family in the war."

I nodded. "She had five children. And her husband was an important man in Nagasaki. When the bomb fell, they all died except her eldest son. It must have been such a blow to her, but she just kept going."

"Yes," said Sachiko, nodding slowly, "I thought something of that nature had happened. And did she always have that noodle shop of hers?"

"No, of course not. Her husband was an important man. That was only afterwards, after she lost everything. Whenever I see her, I think to myself I have to be like her, I should keep looking forward. Because in many ways, she lost more than I did. After all, look at me now. I'm about to start a family of my own."

"Yes, how right you are." The wind had disturbed Sachiko's carefully combed hair. She passed her hand through it, then took a deep breath, "How right you are Etsuko, we shouldn't keep looking back to the past. The war destroyed many things for me, but I still have my daughter. As you say, we have to keep looking forward."

"You know," I said, "it's only in the last few days I've really thought about what it's going to be like. To have a

111

child, I mean. I don't feel nearly so afraid now. I'm going to look forward to it. I'm going to be optimistic from now on."

"And so you should, Etsuko. After all, you have a lot to look forward to. In fact, you'll discover soon enough, it's being a mother that makes life truly worthwhile. What do I care if life is a little dull at my uncle's house? All I want is what's best for my daughter. We'll get her the best private tuition and she'll catch up on her schoolwork in no time. As you say, Etsuko, we must look forward to life."

"I'm so glad you feel like that," I said. "We should both of us be grateful really. We may have lost a lot in the war, but there's still so much to look forward to."

"Yes, Etsuko. There's a lot to look forward to."

Mariko came nearer and stood in front of us. Perhaps she had overheard some of our conversation, for she said to me:

"We're going to live with Yasuko-San again. Did Mother tell you?"

"Yes," I said, "she did. Are you looking forward to living there again, Mariko-San?"

"We might be able to keep the kittens now," the little girl said. "There's plenty of room at Yasuko-San's house."

"We'll have to see about that, Mariko," said Sachiko.

Mariko looked at her mother for a moment. Then she said: "But Yasuko-San likes cats. And anyway, Maru was Yasuko-San's cat before we took her. So the kittens are hers too."

"Yes, Mariko, but we'll have to see. We'll have to see what Yasuko-San's father will say."

The little girl regarded her mother with a sullen look, then turned to me once more. "We might be able to keep them," she said, with a serious expression.

Towards the latter part of the afternoon, we found ourselves back at the clearing where we had first stepped off the cable-car. There still remained in our lunch-boxes some

112

biscuits and chocolates, so we sat down for a snack at one of the picnic tables. At the other end of the clearing, a handful of people were gathered near the metal fence, awaiting the cable-car that would take them back down the mountain.

We had been sitting at the picnic table for several minutes when a voice made us look up. The American woman came striding across the clearing, a broad smile on her face. Without the least sign of bashfulness, she sat down at our table, smiled to us in turn, then began to address Sachiko in English. She was, I supposed, grateful for the chance to communicate other than by means of gestures. Looking around, I spotted the Japanese woman nearby, putting a jacket on her son. She appeared less enthusiastic for our company, but eventually she came towards our table with a smile. She sat down opposite me, and when her son sat beside her, I could see the extent to which mother and child shared the same plump features; most noticeably, their cheeks had a kind of fleshy sagginess to them, not unlike the cheeks of bulldogs. The American woman, all the while, continued to talk loudly to Sachiko.

At the arrival of the strangers, Mariko had opened her sketchbook and begun to draw. The plump-faced woman, after exchanging a few pleasantries with me, turned to the little girl.

"And have you enjoyed your day?" she asked Mariko. "It's very pretty up here, isn't it?"

Mariko continued to crayon her page, not looking up. The woman, however, did not seem in the least deterred.

"What are you drawing there?" she asked. "It looks very nice."

This time, Mariko stopped drawing and looked at the woman coldly.

"That looks very nice. May we see?" The woman reached forward and took the sketchbook. "Aren't these nice, Akira," she said to her son. "Isn't the little lady clever?"

The boy leaned across the table for a better view. He

113

regarded the drawings with interest, but said nothing.

"They're very nice indeed." The woman was turning over the pages. "Did you do all these today?"

Mariko remained silent for a moment. Then she said: "The crayons are new. We bought them this morning. It's harder to draw with new crayons."

"I see. Yes, new crayons are harder, aren't they? Akira here draws too, don't you, Akira?"

"Drawing's easy," the boy said.

"Aren't these nice little pictures, Akira?"

Mariko pointed to the open page. "I don't like that one there. The crayons weren't worn in enough. The one on the next page is better."

"Oh yes. This one's lovely!"

"I did it down at the harbour," said Mariko. "But it was noisy and hot down there, so I hurried."

"But it's very good. Do you enjoy drawing?"

"Yes."

Sachiko and the American woman had both turned towards the sketchbook. The American woman pointed at the drawing and uttered loudly several times the Japanese word for "delicious".

"And what's this?" the plump-faced woman continued. "A butterfly! It must have been very hard to draw it so well. It couldn't have stayed still for very long."

"I remembered it," said Mariko. "I saw one earlier on."

The woman nodded, then turned to Sachiko. "How clever your daughter is. I think it's very commendable for a child to use her memory and imagination. So many children at this age are still copying out of books."

"Yes," said Sachiko. "I suppose so."

I was rather surprised at the dismissiveness of her tone, for she had been talking to the American woman in her most gracious manner. The tubby boy leaned further across the table and put his finger to the page.

"Those ships are too big," he said. "If that's supposed to

114

be a tree, then the ships would be much smaller."

His mother considered this for a moment. "Well, perhaps," she said. "But it's a lovely little drawing all the same. Don't you think so, Akira?"

"The ships are far too big," said the boy.

The woman gave a laugh. "You must excuse Akira," she said to Sachiko. "But you see, he has a quite distinguished tutor for his drawing, and so he's obviously much more discerning about these things than most children his age. Does your daughter have a tutor for her drawing?"

"No, she doesn't." Again, Sachiko's tone was unmistakably cold. The woman, however, appeared to notice nothing.

"It's not a bad idea at all," she went on. "My husband was against it at first. He thought it was quite enough for Akira to have home tuition for maths and science. But I think drawing is important too. A child should develop his imagination while he's young. The teachers at school all agreed with me. But he gets on best with maths. I think maths is very important, don't you?"

"Yes, indeed," said Sachiko. "I'm sure it's very useful."

"Maths sharpens children's minds. You'll find most children good at maths are good at most other things. My husband and I were in no disagreement about getting a maths tutor. And it's been well worth it. Last year, Akira always came third or fourth in his class, but this year he's been top throughout."

"Maths is easy," the boy announced. Then he said to Mariko: "Do you know the nine times table?"

His mother laughed again. "I expect the little lady's very clever too. Her drawing certainly shows promise."

"Maths is easy," the boy said again. "The nine times table is easy as anything."

"Yes, Akira knows all his multiplication now. A lot of children his age only know it up to three or four. Akira, what's nine times five?"

115

"Nine times five make forty-five!"

"And nine times nine?"

"Nine times nine make eighty-one!"

The American woman asked Sachiko something, and when Sachiko nodded she clapped her hands and once more repeated the word "delicious" several times.

"Your daughter seems a bright little lady," the plump-faced woman said to Sachiko. "Does she enjoy school? Akira likes almost everything at school. Apart from maths and drawing, he gets on very well with geography. My friend here was very surprised to find Akira knew the names of all the large cities in America. Weren't you, Suzie-San?" The woman turned to her friend and spoke several faltering words of English. The American woman did not appear to understand, but smiled approvingly towards the boy.

"But maths is Akira's favourite subject. Isn't it, Akira?"

"Maths is easy!"

"And what does the little lady enjoy most at school?" the woman asked, turning again to Mariko.

Mariko did not answer for a moment. Then she said: "I like maths too."

"You like maths too. That's splendid."

"What's nine times six then?" the boy asked her angrily.

"It's so nice when children take an interest in their schoolwork, isn't it?" said his mother.

"Go on, what's nine times six?"

I asked: "What does Akira-San want to do when he grows up?"

"Akira, tell the lady what you're going to become."

"Head Director of Mitsubishi Corporation!"

"His father's firm," his mother explained. "Akira's already very determined."

"Yes, I see," I said, smiling. "How wonderful."

"Who does *your* father work for?" the boy asked Mariko.

"Now, Akira, don't be too inquisitive, it's not nice." The

woman turned to Sachiko again. "A lot of boys his age are still saying they want to be policemen or firemen. But Akira's wanted to work for Mitsubishi since he was much younger."

"Who does *your* father work for?" the boy asked again. This time his mother, instead of intervening, looked towards Mariko expectantly.

"He's a zoo-keeper," said Mariko.

For a brief moment, no one spoke. Curiously, the answer seemed to humble the boy, and he sat back on his bench with a sulky expression. Then his mother said a little uncertainly:

"What an interesting occupation. We're very fond of animals. Is your husband's zoo near here?"

Before Sachiko could reply, Mariko had clambered off the bench noisily. Without a word, she walked away from us, towards a cluster of trees nearby. We all watched her for a moment.

"Is she your eldest?" the woman asked Sachiko.

"I have no others."

"Oh, I see. It's no bad thing really. A child can become more independent that way. I think a child often works harder too. There's six years' difference between this one" — she put her hand on the boy's head — "and the eldest one."

The American woman produced a loud exclamation and clapped her hands. Mariko was progressing steadily up the branches of a tree. The plump-faced woman turned in her seat and looked up at Mariko worriedly.

"Your daughter's quite a tomboy," she said.

The American woman repeated the word "tomboy" gleefully, and clapped her hands again.

"Is it safe?" the plump-faced woman asked. "She might fall."

Sachiko smiled, and her manner towards the woman seemed to grow suddenly warmer. "Are you not used to

117

children climbing trees?" she asked.

The woman continued to watch anxiously. "Are you sure it's safe? A branch may break."

Sachiko gave a laugh. "I'm sure my daughter knows what she's doing. Thank you all the same for your concern. It's so kind of you." She gave the woman an elegant bow. The American woman said something to Sachiko, and they began conversing again in English. The plump-faced woman turned away from the trees.

"Please don't think me impertinent," she said, putting a hand on my arm, "but I couldn't help noticing. Will this be your first time?"

"Yes," I said, with a laugh. "We're expecting it in the autumn."

"How splendid. And your husband, is he also a zoo-keeper?"

"Oh no. He works for an electronics firm."

"Really?"

The woman began to give me advice concerning the care of babies. Meanwhile, I could see over her shoulder the boy wandering away from the table towards Mariko's tree.

"And it's an idea to let the child hear a lot of good music," the woman was saying. "I'm sure that makes a lot of difference. A child should hear good music amongst his earliest sounds."

"Yes, I'm very fond of music."

The boy was standing at the foot of the tree, looking up at Mariko with a puzzled expression.

"Our older son doesn't have as fine an ear for music as Akira," the woman went on. "My husband says this is because he didn't hear enough good music when he was a baby, and I tend to think he's right. In those days, the radio was broadcasting so much military music. I'm sure it did no good at all."

As the woman continued to talk, I could see the boy trying to find a foothold in the tree-trunk. Mariko had come

118

lower and appeared to be advising him. Beside me, the American woman kept laughing loudly, occasionally uttering single words of Japanese. The boy finally managed to hoist himself off the ground; he had one foot pressed into a crevice and was holding on to a branch with both hands. Although only a few centimetres off the ground, he seemed in a state of high tension. It was hard to say if she did so deliberately, but as she lowered herself, the little girl trod firmly on the boy's fingers. The boy gave a shriek, falling clumsily.

The mother turned in alarm. Sachiko and the American woman, neither of whom had seen the incident, also turned towards the fallen boy. He was lying on his side making a loud noise. His mother ran to him and kneeling beside him began to feel his legs. The boy continued his noises. Across the clearing, passengers waiting for the cable-car were all looking our way. After a minute or so, the boy came sobbing to the table, guided by his mother.

"Tree-climbing is so dangerous," the woman said, angrily.

"He didn't fall far," I assured her. "He was hardly on the tree at all."

"He might have broken a bone. I think children should be discouraged from climbing trees. It's so silly."

"She kicked me," the boy sobbed. "She kicked me off the tree. She tried to kill me."

"She kicked you? The little girl kicked you?"

I saw Sachiko cast a glance towards her daughter. Mariko was once more high up the tree.

"She tried to kill me."

"The little girl kicked you?"

"Your son just slipped," I interrupted quickly. "I saw it all. He hardly fell any distance."

"She kicked me. She tried to kill me."

The woman also turned and glanced towards the tree.

"He just slipped," I said again.

119

"You shouldn't be doing such silly things, Akira," the woman said, angrily. "It's very very dangerous to climb trees."

"She tried to kill me."

"You're not to go up trees."

The boy continued to sob.

In Japanese cities, much more so than in England, the restaurant owners, the teahouse proprietors, the shopkeepers all seem to will the darkness to fall; long before the daylight has faded, lanterns appear in the windows, lighted signs above doorways. Nagasaki was already full of the colours of night-time as we came back out into the street that evening; we had left Inasa in the late afternoon and had been eating supper on the restaurant floor of the Hamaya department store. Afterwards, reluctant to end the day, we found ourselves strolling through the sidestreets, in little hurry to reach the tram depot. In those days, I remember it had become the vogue for young couples to be seen in public holding hands — something Jiro and I had never done — and as we walked we saw many such couples seeking their evening's entertainment. The sky, as often on those summer evenings, had become a pale purple colour.

Many of the stalls sold fish, and at that time of the evening, when the fishing boats were coming into the harbour, one would often see men pushing their way through the crowded sidestreets, carrying on their shoulders baskets heavy with freshly caught fish. It was in one such sidestreet, filled with litter and casually strolling people, that we came across the *kujibiki* stand. Since it was never my habit to indulge in *kujibiki* and since it has no equivalents here in England — except perhaps in fairgrounds — I might well have forgotten the existence of such a thing were it not for my memory of that particular evening.

120

We stood at the back of the crowd and watched. A woman was holding up a young boy of around two or three; up on the platform, a man with a handkerchief tied around his head was stooping forward with the bowl so the child could reach. The boy managed to pick out a ticket, but did not seem to know what to do with it. He held it in his hand and looked emptily at the amused faces all around him. The man with the handkerchief bent lower and made some remark to the child which caused the people round about to laugh. In the end, the mother lowered her child, took the ticket from him, and handed it to the man. The ticket won a lipstick, which the woman accepted with a laugh.

Mariko was standing on her tip-toes, trying to see the prizes displayed at the back of the stall. Suddenly she turned to Sachiko and said: "I want to buy a ticket."

"It's rather a waste of money, Mariko."

"I want to buy a ticket." There was a curious urgency in her manner. "I want to try the *kujibiki*."

"Here you are, Mariko-San." I offered her a coin.

She turned to me, a little surprised. Then she took the coin and pushed her way through to the front of the crowd.

A few more contestants tried their luck; a woman won a piece of candy, a middle-aged man won a rubber ball. Then came Mariko's turn.

"Now, little princess," — the man shook the bowl with deliberation — "close your eyes and think hard about that big bear over there."

"I don't want the bear," said Mariko.

The man made a face and the people laughed. "You don't want that big furry bear? Well, well, little princess, what is it you want then?"

Mariko pointed to the back of the stall. "That basket," she said.

"The basket?" The man shrugged. "All right, princess, close your eyes tight and think about your basket. Ready?"

Mariko's ticket won a flowerpot. She came back to where

121

we were standing and handed me her prize.

"Don't you want it?" I asked. "You won it."

"I wanted the basket. The kittens need a basket of their own now."

"Well, never mind."

Mariko turned to her mother. "I want to try once more."

Sachiko sighed. "It's getting late now."

"I want to try. Just once more."

Again, she pushed her way to the platform. As we waited, Sachiko turned to me and said:

"It's funny, but I had a quite different impression of her. Your friend, Mrs Fujiwara, I mean."

"Oh?"

Sachiko leaned her head to see past the spectators. "No, Etsuko," she said, "I'm afraid I never saw her in quite the way you do. Your friend struck me as a woman with nothing left in her life."

"But that's not true," I said.

"Oh? And what does she have to look forward to, Etsuko? What does she have to live for?"

"She has her shop. It's nothing grand, but it means a lot to her."

"Her shop?"

"And she has her son. Her son has a very promising career."

Sachiko was looking again towards the stall. "Yes, I suppose so," she said, with a tired smile. "I suppose she has her son."

This time Mariko won a pencil, and came back to us with a sullen expression. We started to go, but Mariko was still looking towards the Kujibiki stand.

"Come on," Sachiko said. "Etsuko-San needs to be getting home now."

"I want to try once more. Just once more."

Sachiko sighed impatiently, then looked at me. I shrugged and gave a laugh.

122

"All right," said Sachiko. "Try once more."

Several more people won prizes. Once a young woman won a face-compact and the appropriateness of the prize provoked some applause. On seeing Mariko appear for the third time, the man with the handkerchief pulled another of his amusing faces.

"Well, little princess, back again! Still want the basket? Wouldn't you prefer that big furry bear?"

Mariko said nothing, waiting for the man to offer her the bowl. When she had picked out a ticket, the man examined it closely, then glanced behind him to where the prizes were exhibited. He scrutinized the ticket once more, then finally gave a nod.

"You haven't won the basket. But you have won — a *major prize!*"

There was laughter and applause all around. The man went to the back of the stall and returned with what looked like a large wooden box.

"For your mother to keep her vegetables in!" he announced — to the crowd rather than to Mariko — and for a brief moment held up the prize. Beside me, Sachiko burst into laughter and joined in the applause. A gangway formed to allow Mariko through with her prize.

Sachiko was still laughing as we came away from the crowd. She had laughed so much that small tears had appeared in her eyes; she wiped them away and looked at the box.

"Whata strange-lookingthing," shesaid,passingittome.

It was the size of an orange box and surprisingly light; the wood was smooth but unvarnished, and on one side were two sliding panels of wire gauze.

"It may come in useful," I said, sliding open a panel.

"I won a major prize," said Mariko.

"Yes, well done," Sachiko said.

"I won a kimono once," Mariko said to me. "In Tokyo, I won a kimono once."

"Well, you've won again."

"Etsuko, perhaps you could carry my bag. Then I could carry this object home."

"I won a major prize," said Mariko.

"Yes, you were very good," said her mother, and laughed a little.

We walked away from the *kujibiki* stand. The street was littered with discarded newspapers and all manner of rubbish.

"The kittens could live in there, couldn't they?" Mariko said. "We could put rugs inside it and that could be their house."

Sachiko looked doubtfully at the box in her arms. "I'm not sure they'd like it so much."

"That could be their house. Then when we go to Yasuko-San's house, we could carry them in there."

Sachiko smiled tiredly.

"We could, couldn't we, Mother? We could carry the kittens in there."

"Yes, I suppose so," said Sachiko. "Yes, all right. We'll carry the kittens in there."

"So we can keep the kittens then?"

"Yes, we can keep the kittens. I'm sure Yasuko-San's father won't object."

Mariko ran a little way ahead, then waited for us to catch up.

"So we won't have to find homes for them any more?"

"No, not now. We're going to Yasuko-San's house, so we'll keep the kittens after all."

"We won't have to find owners then. We can keep them all. We could take them in the box, couldn't we, Mother?"

"Yes," said Sachiko. Then she tossed back her head and once more began to laugh.

I often find myself recalling Mariko's face the way I saw it that evening on the tram going home. She was staring out of the window, her forehead pressed against the glass; a boyish face, caught in the changing lights of the city rattling by outside. Mariko remained silent throughout that journey home, and Sachiko and I conversed little. Once, I remember, Sachiko asked:

"Will your husband be angry with you?"

"Quite possibly," I said, with a smile. "But I did warn him yesterday I might be late."

"It's been an enjoyable day."

"Yes. Jiro will just have to sit and get angry. I've enjoyed today very much."

"We must do it again, Etsuko."

"Yes, we must."

"Remember, won't you, to come and visit me after I move."

"Yes, I'll remember."

We fell silent again after that. It was a little later, just as the tram slowed for a stop, I felt Sachiko give a sudden start. She was looking down the carriage, to where two or three people had gathered near the exit. A woman was standing there looking at Mariko. She was around thirty or so, with a thin face and tired expression. It was conceivable she was gazing at Mariko quite innocently, and but for Sachiko's reaction I doubt if my suspicions would have been aroused. In the meantime, Mariko continued to look out of the window, quite unaware of the woman.

The woman noticed Sachiko looking at her and turned away. The tram came to a stop, the doors opened and the woman stepped out.

"Did you know that person?" I asked, quietly.

Sachiko laughed a little. "No. I just made a mistake."

"You mistook her for someone else?"

"Just for a moment. There wasn't even a resemblance really." She laughed again, then glanced outside to check where we were.

Chapter Eight

In retrospect it seems quite clear why Ogata-San remained with us for as long as he did that summer. Knowing his son well enough, he must have recognized Jiro's strategy over the matter concerning Shigeo Matsuda's magazine article; my husband was simply waiting for Ogata-San to return home to Fukuoka so the whole affair could be forgotten. Meanwhile, he would continue to agree readily that such an attack on the family name should be dealt with both promptly and firmly, that the matter was his concern as much as his father's, and that he would write to his old schoolfriend as soon as he had time. I can see now, with hindsight, how typical this was of the way Jiro faced any potentially awkward confrontation. Had he not, years later, faced another crisis in much the same manner, it may be that I would never have left Nagasaki. However, that is by the way.

I have recounted earlier some details of the evening my husband's two drunken colleagues arrived to interrupt the chess game between Jiro and Ogata-San. That night, as I prepared for bed, I felt a strong urge to talk to Jiro about the whole business concerning Shigeo Matsuda; while I did not wish Jiro to write such a letter against his will, I was feeling more and more keenly that he should make his position clearer to his father. As it was, however, I refrained from mentioning the subject that night, just as I had done on previous occasions. For one thing, my husband would have considered it no business of mine to comment on such a matter. Furthermore, at that time of night, Jiro was invariably tired and any attempts to converse would only make him impatient. And in any case, it was never in the nature of our relationship to discuss such things openly.

Throughout the following day, Ogata-San remained in the apartment, often studying the chess game which — so he told me — had been interrupted at a crucial stage the previous night. Then that evening, an hour or so after we had finished supper, he brought out the chess-board again and began once more to study the pieces. Once, he looked up and said to my husband:

"So, Jiro. Tomorrow's the big day then."

Jiro looked up from his newspaper and gave a short laugh. "It's nothing to make a fuss about," he said.

"Nonsense. It's a big day for you. Of couse, it's imperative you do your best for the firm, but in my view this is a triumph in itself, whatever the outcome tomorrow. To be asked to represent the firm at this level, so early in your career, that can't be usual, even these days."

Jiro gave a shrug. "I suppose not. Of course, even if tomorrow goes exceptionally well, that's no guarantee I'll get the promotion. But I suppose the manager must be reasonably pleased with my efforts this year."

"I should think he has great faith in you, by all accounts. And how do you think it will go tomorrow?"

"Smoothly enough, I should hope. At this stage all the parties involved need to co-operate. It's more a case of laying the groundwork for the real negotiations in the autumn. It's nothing so special."

"Well, we'll have to just wait and see how it goes. Now, Jiro, why don't we finish off this game. We've been at it for three days."

"Oh yes, the game. Of course, Father, you realize however successful I am tomorrow, that's no guarantee I'll be given the promotion."

"Of course not, Jiro, I realize these things. I came up through a competitive career myself. I know only too well

127

how it is. Sometimes others are chosen in preference who by all rights shouldn't even be considered your equals. But you mustn't let such things deter you. You persevere and triumph in the end. Now, how about finishing off this game."

My husband glanced towards the chess-board, but showed no sign of moving nearer it. "You'd just about won, if I remember," he said.

"Well, you're in quite a difficult corner, but there's a way out if you can find it. Do you remember, Jiro, when I first taught you this game, how I always warned you about using the castles too early? And you still make the same mistake. Do you see?"

"The castles, yes. As you say."

"And incidentally, Jiro, I don't think you're thinking your moves out in advance, are you? Do you remember how much trouble I once took to make you plan at least three moves ahead. But I don't think you've been doing that."

"Three moves ahead? Well, no, I suppose I haven't. I can't claim to be an expert like yourself, Father. In any case, I think we can say you've won."

"In fact, Jiro, it became painfully obvious very early in the game, that you weren't thinking your moves out. How often have I told you? A good chess player needs to think ahead, three moves on at the very least."

"Yes, I suppose so."

"For instance, why did you move this horse here? Jiro, look, you're not even looking. Can you even remember why you moved this here?"

Jiro glanced towards the board. "To be honest, I don't remember," he said. "There was probably a good enough reason at the time."

"A good enough reason? What nonsense, Jiro. For the first few moves, you were planning ahead, I could see that. You actually had a strategy then. But as soon as I broke that

128

down, you gave up, you began playing one move at a time. Don't you remember what I always used to tell you? Chess is all about maintaining coherent strategies. It's about not giving up when the enemy destroys one plan, but to immediately come up with the next. A game isn't won and lost at the point when the king is finally cornered. The game's sealed when a player gives up having any strategy at all. When his soldiers are all scattered, they have no common cause, and they move one piece at a time, that's when you've lost."

"Very well, Father, I admit it. I've lost. Now perhaps we can forget about it."

Ogata-San glanced towards me, then back at Jiro. "Now what kind of talk is that? I studied this board quite hard today and I can see three separate means by which you can escape."

My husband lowered his newspaper. "Forgive me if I'm mistaken," he said, "but I believe you just said yourself, the player who cannot maintain a coherent strategy is inevitably the loser. Well, as you've pointed out so repeatedly, I've been thinking only one move at a time, so there seems little point in carrying on. Now if you'll excuse me, I'd like to finish reading this report."

"Why, Jiro, this is sheer defeatism. The game's far from lost, I've just told you. You should be planning your defence now, to survive and fight me again. Jiro, you always had a streak of defeatism in you, ever since you were young. I'd hoped I'd taken it out of you, but here it is again, after all this time."

"Forgive me, but I fail to see what defeatism has to do with it. This is merely a game . . ."

"It may indeed be just a game. But a father gets to know his son well enough. A father can recognize these unwelcome traits when they arise. This is hardly a quality I'm proud of in you, Jiro. You gave up as soon as your first strategy collapsed. And now when you're forced on to the

129

defensive, you sulk and don't want to play the game any more. Why, this is just the way you were at nine years old."

"Father, this is all nonsense. I have better things to do than think about chess all day."

Jiro had spoken quite loudly, and for a moment Ogata-San looked somewhat taken aback.

"It may be very well for you, Father," my husband continued. "You have the whole day to dream up your strategies and ploys. Personally, I have better things to do with my time."

With that, my husband returned to his paper. His father continued to stare at him, an astonished look on his face. Then finally, Ogata-San began to laugh.

"Come, Jiro," he said, "we're shouting at each other like a pair of fishermen's wives." He gave another laugh. "Like a pair of fishermen's wives."

Jiro did not look up.

"Come on, Jiro, let's stop our argument. If you don't want to finish the game, we don't have to finish it."

My husband still gave no sign of having heard.

Ogata-San laughed again. "All right, you win. We won't play any more. But let me show you how you could have got out of this little corner here. There's three things you could have done. The first one's the most simple and there's little I could have done about it. Look, Jiro, look here. Jiro, look, I'm showing you something."

Jiro continued to ignore his father. He had all the appearance of someone solemnly absorbed in his reading. He turned over a page and carried on reading.

Ogata-San nodded to himself, laughing quietly. "Just like when he was a child," he said. "When he doesn't get his own way, he sulks and there's nothing to be done with him." He glanced towards where I was sitting and laughed rather oddly. Then he turned back to his son. "Jiro, look. Let me show you this at least. It's simplicity itself."

Quite suddenly, my husband flung down his news-

130

paper and made a movement towards his father. Clearly, what he had intended was to knock the chess-board across the floor and all the pieces with it. But he moved clumsily and before he could strike the board, his foot had upset the teapot beside him. The pot rolled on to its side, the lid fell open with a rattle, and the tea ran swiftly across the surface of the tatami. Jiro, not sure what had occurred, turned and stared at the spilt tea. Then he turned back and glared at the chess-board. The sight of the chessmen, still upright on their squares, seemed to anger him all the more, and for a moment I thought he would make another attempt to upset them. As it was, he got to his feet, snatched up his newspaper, and left the room without a word.

I went over quickly to where the tea had spilt. Some of the liquid had begun to soak into the cushion Jiro had been sitting on. I moved the cushion and rubbed at it with the edge of my apron.

"Just like he used to be," Ogata-San said. A faint smile had appeared around his eyes. "Children become adults but they don't change much."

I went out into the kitchen and found a cloth. When I returned, Ogata-San was sitting just as I had left him, the smile still hovering around his eyes. He was gazing at the puddle on the tatami and looked deep in thought. Indeed, he seemed so absorbed by the sight of the tea, I hesitated a little before kneeling down to wipe it away.

"You mustn't let this upset you, Etsuko," he said, eventually. "It's nothing to upset yourself about."

"No." I continued to wipe the tatami.

"Well, I suppose we might as well turn in fairly soon. It's good to turn in early once in a while."

"Yes."

"You mustn't let this upset you, Etsuko. Jiro will have forgotten the whole thing by tomorrow, you'll see. I remember these spells of his very well. In fact, it makes you quite nostalgic, witnessing a little scene like that. It

131

reminds me so much of when he was small. Yes, it's enough to make you quite nostalgic."

I continued to wipe away the tea.

"Now, Etsuko," he said. "This is nothing to upset yourself about."

I exchanged no further words with my husband until the following morning. He ate his breakfast glancing occasionally at the morning newspaper I had placed beside his bowl. He spoke little and made no comment on the fact that his father had not yet emerged. For my part, I listened carefully for sounds from Ogata-San's room, but could hear nothing.

"I hope it all goes well today," I said, after we had sat in silence for some minutes.

My husband gave a shrug. "It's nothing to make a fuss about," he said. Then he looked up at me and said: "I wanted my black silk tie today, but you seem to have done something with it. I wish you wouldn't meddle with my ties."

"The black silk one? It's hanging on the rail with your other ties."

"It wasn't there just now. I wish you'd stop meddling with them all the time."

"The silk one should be there with the others," I said. "I ironed it the day before yesterday, because I knew you'd be wanting it for today, but I made sure to put it back. Are you sure it wasn't there?"

My husband sighed impatiently and looked down at the newspaper. "It doesn't matter," he said. "This one will have to do."

He continued to eat in silence. Meanwhile, there was still no sign of Ogata-San and eventually I rose to my feet and went to listen outside his door. When after several seconds I had not heard a sound, I was about to slide open the door a little way. But my husband turned and said:

132

"What are you up to? I haven't got all morning, you know." He pushed his teacup forward.

I seated myself again, put his used dishes away to one side, and poured him some tea. He sipped it rapidly, glancing over the front page of the newspaper.

"This is an important day for us," I said. "I hope it goes well."

"It's nothing to make such a fuss about," he said, not looking up.

However, before he left that morning, Jiro studied himself carefully in the mirror by the entryway, adjusting his tie and examining his jaw to check he had shaved efficiently. When he had left, I went over once more to Ogata-San's door and listened. I still could hear nothing.

"Father?" I called softly.

"Ah, Etsuko," I heard Ogata-San's voice from within. "I might have known you wouldn't let me lie in."

Somewhat relieved, I went to the kitchen to prepare a fresh pot of tea, then laid the table ready for Ogata-San's breakfast. When he eventually sat down to eat, he remarked casually:

"Jiro's left already, I suppose."

"Oh yes, he went a long time ago. I was just about to throw Father's breakfast away. I thought he'd be far too lazy to get up much before noon."

"Now, don't be cruel, Etsuko. When you get to my age, you like to relax once in a while. Besides, this is like a vacation for me, staying here with you."

"Well, I suppose just this once then, Father can be forgiven for being so lazy."

"I won't get the opportunity to lie in like this once I get back to Fukuoka," he said, taking up his chopsticks. Then he sighed deeply. "I suppose it's time I was getting back soon."

"Getting back? But there's no hurry, Father."

"No, I really have to be getting back soon. There's plenty

133

of work to be getting on with."

"Work? What work is that?"

"Well, for a start, I need to build new panels for the veranda. Then there's the rockery. I haven't even started on it yet. The stones were delivered months ago and they've just been sitting there in the garden waiting for me." he gave a sigh and began to eat. "I certainly won't get to lie in like this once I get back."

"But there's no need to go just yet, is there, Father? Your rockery can wait a little longer."

"You're very kind, Etsuko. But time's pressing on now. You see, I'm expecting my daughter and her husband down again this autumn, and I'll need to get all this work finished before they come. Last year and the year before, they came to see me in the autumn. So I rather suspect they'll want to come again this year."

"I see."

"Yes, they're bound to want to come again this autumn. It's the most convenient time for Kikuko's husband. And Kikuko's always saying in her letters how curious she is to see my new house."

Ogata-San nodded to himself, then carried on eating from his bowl. I watched him for a while.

"What a loyal daughter Kikuko-San is to you, Father," I said. "It's a long way to come, all that way from Osaka. She must miss you."

"I suppose she feels the need to get away from her father-in-law once in a while. I can't think why else she would want to come so far."

"How unkind, Father. I'm sure she misses you. I'll have to tell her what you're saying."

Ogata-San laughed. "But it's true. Old Watanabe rules over them like a war-lord. Whenever they come down, they're forever talking about how intolerable he's getting. Personally I rather like the old man, but there's no denying he's an old war-lord. I expect they'd like some place like

134

this, Etsuko, an apartment like this just to themselves. It's no bad thing, young couples living away from the parents. More and more couples do it now. Young people don't want overbearing old men ruling over them for ever."

Ogata-San seemed to remember the food in his bowl and began to eat hurriedly. When he had finished, he got to his feet and went over to the window. For a moment he stood there, his back to me, looking at the view. Then he adjusted the window to let in more air, and took a deep breath.

"Are you pleased with your new house, Father?" I asked.

"My house? Why, yes. It'll need a little more work here and there, as I say. But it's much more compact. The Nagasaki house was far too large for just one old man."

He continued to gaze out of the window; in the sharp morning light, all I could see of his head and shoulders was a hazy outline.

"But it was a nice house, the old house," I said. "I still stop and look at it if I'm walking that way. In fact, I went past it last week on my way back from Mrs Fujiwara's."

I thought he had not heard me, for he continued to gaze silently out at the view. But a moment later, he said:

"And how did it look, the old house?"

"Oh, much the same. The new occupants must like it the way Father left it."

He turned towards me slightly. "And what about the azaleas, Etsuko? Were the azaleas still in the gateway?" The brightness still prevented me from seeing his face clearly, but I supposed from his voice that he was smiling.

"Azaleas?"

"Well, I suppose there's no reason why you should remember." He turned back to the window and stretched out his arms. "I planted them in the gateway that day. The day it was all finally decided."

"The day what was decided?"

"That you and Jiro were to be married. But I never told you about the azaleas, so I suppose it's rather unreasonable

135

of me to expect you to remember about them."

"You planted some azaleas for me? Now that was a nice thought. But no, I don't think you ever mentioned it."

"But you see, Etsuko, you asked for them." He had turned towards me again. "In fact, you positively ordered me to plant them in the gateway."

"What? — I laughed — "I ordered you?"

"Yes, you ordered me. Like I was some hired gardener. Don't you remember? Just when I thought it was all settled at last, and you were finally to become my daughter-in-law, you told me there was one thing more, you wouldn't live in a house without azaleas in the gateway. And if I didn't plant azaleas then the whole thing would be called off. So what could I do? I went straight out and planted azaleas."

I laughed a little. "Now you mention it," I said, "I remember something like that. But what nonsense, Father. I never forced you."

"Oh yes, you did, Etsuko. You said you wouldn't live in a house without azaleas in the gateway." He came away from the window and sat down opposite me again. "Yes, Etsuko," he said "just like a hired gardener."

We both laughed and I began to pour out the tea.

"Azaleas were always my favourite flowers, you see," I said.

"Yes. So you said."

I finished pouring and we sat silently for a few moments, watching the steam rise from the teacups.

"And I had no idea then," I said. "About Jiro's plans, I mean."

"No."

I reached forward and placed a plate of small cakes by his teacup. Ogata-San regarded them with a smile. Eventually, he said:

"The azaleas came up beautifully. But by that time, of course, you'd moved away. Still, it's no bad thing at all, young couples living on their own. Look at Kikuko and her

136

husband. They'd love to have a little place of their own, but old Watanabe won't even let them consider it. What an old war-lord he is."

"Now I think of it," I said, "there *were* azaleas in the gateway last week. The new occupants must agree with me. Azaleas are essential for a gateway."

"I'm glad they're still there." Ogata-San took a sip from his teacup. Then he sighed and said with a laugh: "What an old war-lord that Watanabe is."

Shortly after breakfast, Ogata-San suggested we should go and look around Nagasaki — "like the tourists do", as he put it. I agreed at once and we took a tram into the city. As I recall, we spent some time at an art gallery, and then, a little before noon, we went to visit the peace memorial in the large public park not far from the centre of the city.

The park was commonly known as "Peace Park" — I never discovered whether this was the official name — and indeed, despite the sounds of children and birds, an atmosphere of solemnity hung over that large expanse of green. The usual adornments, such as shrubs and fountains, had been kept to a minimum, and the effect was a kind of austerity; the flat grass, a wide summer sky, and the memorial itself — a massive white statue in memory of those killed by the atomic bomb — presiding over its domain.

The statue resembled some muscular Greek god, seated with both arms outstretched. With his right hand, he pointed to the sky from where the bomb had fallen; with his other arm — stretched out to his left — the figure was supposedly holding back the forces of evil. His eyes were closed in prayer.

It was always my feeling that the statue had a rather cumbersome appearance, and I was never able to associate it with what had occurred that day the bomb had fallen, and those terrible days which followed. Seen from a distance, the figure looked almost comical, resembling a policeman conducting traffic. It remained for me nothing more than a statue, and while most people in Nagasaki seemed to appreciate it as some form of gesture, I suspect the general feeling was much like mine. And today, should I by chance recall that large white statue in Nagasaki, I find myself reminded primarily of my visit to Peace Park with Ogata-San that morning, and that business concerning his postcard.

"It doesn't look quite so impressive in a picture," I remember Ogata-San saying, holding up the postcard of the statue which he had just bought. We were standing some fifty yards or so from the monument. "I've been meaning to send a card for some time," he continued. "I'll be going back to Fukuoka any day now, but I suppose it's still worth sending. Etsuko, do you have a pen? Perhaps I should send it straight away, otherwise I'm bound to forget."

I found a pen in my handbag and we sat down on a bench nearby. I became curious when I noticed him staring at the blank side of the card, his pen poised but not writing. Once or twice, I saw him glance up towards the statue as if for inspiration. Finally I asked him:

"Are you sending it to a friend in Fukuoka?"

"Well, just an acquaintance."

"Father's looking very guilty," I said. "I wonder who it can be he's writing to."

Ogata-San glanced up with a look of astonishment. Then he burst into loud laughter. "Guilty? Am I really?"

"Yes, very guilty. I wonder what Father gets up to when there's no one to keep an eye on him."

Ogata-San continued to laugh loudly. He was laughing so much I could feel the bench shake. He recovered a little and said: "Very well, Etsuko. You've caught me. You've caught me writing to my *girl-friend* — he used the English word. "Caught me red-handed." He began laughing again.

"I always suspected Father led a glamorous life in Fukuoka."

"Yes, Etsuko" — he was still laughing a little — "a very glamorous life." Then he took a deep breath and looked down once more at his postcard. "You know, I really don't know what to write. Perhaps I could just send it with nothing written. After all, I only wanted to show her what the memorial looks like. But then again, perhaps that's rather too informal."

"Well, I can't advise you, Father, unless you reveal who this mysterious lady is."

"The mysterious lady, Etsuko, runs a small restaurant in Fukuoka. It's quite near my house so I usually go there for my evening meals. I talk to her sometimes, she's pleasant enough, and I promised I'd send her a postcard of the peace memorial. I'm afraid that's all there is to it."

"I see, Father. But I'm still suspicious."

"Quite a pleasant old woman, but she gets tiresome after a while. If I'm the only customer, she stands and talks all through the meal. Unfortunately there aren't many other suitable places to eat nearby. You see, Etsuko, if you'd teach me to cook, as you promised, then I wouldn't need to suffer the likes of her."

"But it would be pointless," I said, laughing. "Father would never get the hang of it."

"Nonsense. You're simply afraid I'll surpass you. It's most selfish of you, Etsuko. Now let me see" — he looked at his postcard once more — "What can I say to the old lady?"

"Do you remember Mrs Fujiwara?" I asked. "She runs a noodle shop now. Near Father's old house."

"Yes, so I hear. A great pity. Someone of her position running a noodle shop."

"But she enjoys it. It gives her something to work for. She often asks after you."

139

"A great pity," he said again. "Her husband was a distinguished man. I had much respect for him. And now she's running a noodle shop. Extraordinary." He shook his head gravely. "I'd call in and pay my respects, but then I suppose she'd find that rather awkward. In her present circumstances, I mean."

"Father, she's not ashamed to be running a noodle shop. She's proud of it. She says she always wanted to run a business, however humble. I expect she'd be delighted if you called on her."

"Her shop is in Nakagawa, you say?"

"Yes. Quite near the old house."

Ogata-San seemed to consider this for some time. Then he turned to me and said: "Right, then, Etsuko. Let's go and pay her a visit." He scribbled quickly on the postcard and gave me back the pen.

"You mean, go now, Father?" I was a little taken aback by his sudden decisiveness.

"Yes, why not?"

"Very well. I suppose she could give us lunch."

"Yes, perhaps. But I've no wish to humiliate the good lady."

"She'd be pleased to give us lunch."

Ogata-San nodded and for a moment did not speak. Then he said with some deliberation: "As a matter of fact, Etsuko, I'd been thinking of visiting Nakagawa for some time now. I'd like to call in on a certain person there."

"Oh?"

"I wonder if he'd be in at this time of day."

"Who is it you wish to call on, Father?"

"Shigeo. Shigeo Matsuda. I've been intending to pay him a call for some time. Perhaps he takes his lunch at home, in which case I may just catch him. That would be preferable to disturbing him at his school."

For a few minutes, Ogata-San gazed towards the statue, a slightly puzzled look on his face. I remained silent, watching the postcard he was rotating in his hands. Then suddenly he slapped his knees and stood up.

"Right, Etsuko," he said, "let's do that then. We'll try Shigeo first, then we could call in on Mrs Fujiwara."

It must have been around noon that we boarded the tram to take us to Nakagawa; the car was stiflingly crowded and the streets outside were filled with the lunchtime hordes. But as we came away from the city centre, the passengers became more sparse, and by the time the car reached its terminus at Nakagawa, there were only a handful of us left. Stepping out of the tram, Ogata-San paused for a moment and stroked his chin. It was not easy to tell whether he was savouring the feeling of being back in the district, or whether he was simply trying to remember the way to Shigeo Matsuda's house. We were standing in a concrete yard surrounded by several empty tram cars. Above our heads, a maze of black wires crossed the air. The sun was shining down with some force, causing the painted surfaces of the cars to gleam sharply.

"What heat," Ogata-San remarked, wiping his forehead. Then he began to walk, leading the way towards a row of houses which began on the far side of the tram yard.

The district had not changed greatly over the years. As we walked, the narrow roads twisted, climbed and fell. Houses, many of them still familiar to me, stood wherever the hilly landscape would permit; some were perched precariously on slopes, others squeezed into unlikely corners. Blankets and laundry hung from many of the balconies. We walked on, past other houses more grand-looking, but we passed neither Ogata-San's old house nor the house I had once lived in with my parents. In fact, the thought occurred to me that perhaps Ogata-San had chosen a route so as to deliberately avoid them.

I doubt if we walked for much more than ten or fifteen

minutes in all, but the sun and the steep hills became very tiring. Eventually we stopped halfway up a steep path, and Ogata-San ushered me underneath the shelter of a leafy tree that hung over the pavement. Then he pointed across the road to a pleasant-looking old house with large sloping roof-tiles in the traditional manner.

"That's Shigeo's place," he said. "I knew his father quite well. As far as I know, his mother still lives with him." Then Ogata-San began to stroke his chin, just as he had done on first stepping off the tram. I said nothing and waited.

"Quite possibly he won't be home," said Ogata-San. "He'll probably spend the lunch break in the staff room with his colleagues."

I continued to wait silently. Ogata-San remained standing beside me, gazing at the house. Finally, he said:

"Etsuko, how far is it to Mrs Fujiwara's from here? Have you any idea?"

"It's just a few minutes' walk."

"Now I think of it, perhaps it may be best if you went on ahead, and I could meet you there. That may be the best thing."

"Very well. If that's what you wish."

"In fact, this was all very inconsiderate of me."

"I'm not an invalid, Father."

He laughed quickly, then glanced again towards the house. "I think it might be best," he said again. "You go on ahead."

"Very well."

"I don't expect to be long. In fact" — he glanced once more towards the house — "in fact, why don't you wait here until I pull the bell. If you see me go in, then you can go on to Mrs Fujiwara's. This has all been very inconsiderate of me."

"It's perfectly all right, Father. Now listen carefully, or else you'll never find the noodle shop. You remember

142

where the doctor used to have his surgery?"

But Ogata-San was no longer listening. Across the road, the entrance gate had slid open, and a thin young man with spectacles had appeared. He was dressed in his shirt-sleeves and held a small briefcase under his arm. He squinted a little as he stepped further into the glare, then bent over the briefcase and began searching through it. Shigeo Matsuda looked thinner and more youthful than I remembered him from the few occasions I had met him in the past.

Chapter Nine

Shigeo Matsuda tied the buckle of his briefcase, then glancing about him with a distracted air came walking over to our side of the road. For a brief moment he glanced our way but, not recognizing us, went walking on.

Ogata-San watched him go by. Then when the young man had gone several yards down the road, he called out: "Ah, Shigeo!"

Shigeo Matsuda stopped and turned. Then he came towards us with a puzzled look.

"How are you, Shigeo?"

The young man peered through his spectacles, then burst into cheerful laughter.

"Why, Ogata-San! Now this is an unexpected surprise!" He bowed and held out his hand. "What a splendid surprise. Why Etsuko-San too! How are you? How nice to meet again."

We exchanged bows, and he shook hands with us both. Then he said to Ogata-San:

"Were you by any chance about to visit me? This is bad luck, my lunch break's almost over now." He glanced at his watch. "But we could go back inside for a few minutes."

"No, no," said Ogata-San hurriedly. "Don't let us interrupt your work. It just so happened we were passing this way, and I remembered you lived here. I was just pointing out your house to Etsuko."

"Please, I can spare a few minutes. Let me offer you some tea at least. It's a sweltering day out here."

"No, no. You must get to work."

For a moment the two men stood looking at each other.

"And how is everything, Shigeo?" Ogata-San asked. "How are things at the school?"

"Oh, much the same as ever. You know how it is. And you, Ogata-San, you're enjoying your retirement, I hope? I had no idea you were in Nagasaki. Jiro and I seem to have lost touch these days." Then he turned to me and said: "I'm always meaning to write, but I'm so forgetful."

I smiled and made some polite comment. Then the two men looked at each other again.

"You're looking splendidly well, Ogata-San," Shigeo Matsuda said. "You find Fukuoka to your liking?"

"Yes, a fine city. My hometown, you know."

"Really?"

There was another pause. Then Ogata-San said: "Please don't let us keep you. If you have to hurry away, I quite understand."

"No, no. I have a few minutes yet. A pity you weren't passing a little earlier. Perhaps you'd care to call in before you leave Nagasaki."

"Yes, I'll try to. But there's so many people to visit."

"Yes, I can understand how it is."

"And your mother, is she well?"

"Yes, she's fine. Thank you."

For a moment, they fell silent again.

"I'm glad everything's going well," Ogata-San said, eventually. "Yes, we were just passing this way and I was telling Etsuko-San you lived here. In fact, I was just remembering how you used to come and play with Jiro, when you were both little boys."

Shigeo Matsuda laughed. "Time really flies by, doesn't it?" he said.

"Yes. I was just saying as much to Etsuko. In fact, I was just about to tell her about a curious little thing. I happened to remember it, when I saw your house. A curious little thing."

145

"Oh yes?"

"Yes. I just happened to remember it when I saw your house, that's all. You see, I was reading something the other day. An article in a journal. The *New Education Digest*, I think it was called."

The young man said nothing for a moment, then he adjusted his position on the pavement and put down his briefcase.

"I see," he said.

"I was rather surprised to read it. In fact, I was quite astonished."

"Yes. I suppose you would be."

"It was quite extraordinary, Shigeo. Quite extra-ordinary."

Shigeo Matsuda took a deep breath and looked down at the ground. He nodded, but said nothing.

"I'd meant to come and speak to you for some days now," Ogata-San continued. "But of course, the matter slipped my mind. Shigeo, tell me honestly, do you believe a word of what you wrote? Explain to me what made you write such things. Explain it to me, Shigeo, then I can go home to Fukuoka with my mind at rest. At the moment, I'm very puzzled."

Shigeo Matsuda was prodding a pebble with the end of his shoe. Finally he sighed, looked up at Ogata-San and adjusted his spectacles.

"Many things have changed over the last few years," he said.

"Well, of course they have. I can see that much. What kind of answer is that, Shigeo?"

"Ogata-San, let me explain." He paused and looked down at the ground again. For a second or two, he scratched at his ear. "You see, you must understand. Many things have changed now. And things are changing still. We live in a different age from those days when . . . when you were an influential figure."

"But, Shigeo, what has this to do with anything? Things may change, but why write such an article? Have I ever done something to offend you?"

"No, never. At least, not to me personally."

"I should think not. Do you remember the day I introduced you to the principal at your school? That wasn't so long ago, was it? Or was that perhaps a different era too?"

"Ogata-San" — Shigeo Matsuda had raised his voice, and an air of authority seemed to enter his manner — "Ogata-San, I only wish you'd called in an hour earlier. Then perhaps I'd have been able to explain at greater length. There isn't time to talk the whole thing over now. But let me just say this much. Yes, I believed everything I wrote in that article and still do. In your day, children in Japan were taught terrible things. They were taught lies of the most damaging kind. Worst of all, they were taught not to see, not to question. And that's why the country was plunged into the most evil disaster in her entire history."

"We may have lost the war," Ogata-San interrupted, "but that's no reason to ape the ways of the enemy. We lost the war because we didn't have enough guns and tanks, not because our people were cowardly, not because our society was shallow. You have no idea, Shigeo, how hard we worked, men like myself, men like Dr Endo, whom you also insulted in your article. We cared deeply for the country and worked hard to ensure the correct values were preserved and handed on."

"I don't doubt these things. I don't doubt you were sincere and hard working. I've never questioned that for one moment. But it just so happens that your energies were spent in a misguided direction, an evil direction. You weren't to know this, but I'm afraid it's true. It's all behind us now and we can only be thankful."

"This is extraordinary, Shigeo. Can you really believe this? Who taught you to say such things?"

"Ogata-San, be honest with yourself. In your heart of

147

hearts, you must know yourself what I'm saying is true. And to be fair, you shouldn't be blamed for not realizing the true consequences of your actions. Very few men could see where it was all leading at the time, and those men were put in prison for saying what they thought. But they're free now, and they'll lead us to a new dawn."

"A new dawn? What nonsense is this?"

"Now, I must be on my way. I'm sorry we couldn't discuss this any longer."

"What is this, Shigeo? How can you say these things? You obviously have no idea of the effort and devotion men like Dr Endo gave to their work. You were just a small boy then, how could you know how things were? How can you know what we gave and what we achieved?"

"As a matter of fact, I do happen to be familiar with certain aspects of your career. For instance, the sacking and imprisoning of the five teachers at Nishizaka. April of 1938, if I'm not mistaken. But those men are free now, and they'll help us reach a new dawn. Now please excuse me." He picked up his briefcase and bowed to us in turn. "My regards to Jiro," he added, then turned and walked away.

Ogata-San watched the young man disappear down the hill. He continued to stand there for several more moments, not speaking. Then when he turned to me, there was a smile around his eyes.

"How confident young men are," he said. "I suppose I was much the same once. Very sure of my opinions."

"Father," I said. "Perhaps we should go and see Mrs Fujiwara now. It's time we ate lunch."

"Why, of course, Etsuko. This is very inconsiderate of me, making you stand about in this heat. Yes, let's go and see the good lady. I'll be very pleased to see her again."

We made our way down the hill, then crossed a wooden bridge over a narrow river. Below us, children were playing along the riverbank, some with fishing poles. Once, I said to Ogata-San:

148

"What nonsense he was speaking."

"Who? You mean Shigeo?"

"What vile nonsense. I don't think you should pay the slightest attention, Father."

Ogata-San laughed, but made no reply.

As always at that hour, the shopping area of the district was busy with people. On entering the shaded forecourt of the noodle shop, I was pleased to see several of the tables occupied with customers. Mrs Fujiwara saw us and came across the forecourt.

"Why, Ogata-San," she exclaimed, recognizing him immediately, "how splendid to see you again. It's been a long time, hasn't it?"

"A long time indeed." Ogata-San returned the bow Mrs Fujiwara gave him. "Yes, a long time."

I was struck by the warmth with which they greeted each other, for as far as I knew Ogata-San and Mrs Fujiwara had never known one another well. They exchanged what seemed an endless succession of bows, before Mrs Fujiwara went to fetch us something to eat.

She returned presently with two steaming bowls, apologizing that she had nothing better for us. Ogata-San bowed appreciatively and began to eat.

"I thought you'd have forgotten me long ago, Mrs Fujiwara," he remarked with a smile. "Indeed, it's been a long time."

"It's such a pleasure to meet again like this," Mrs Fujiwara said, seating herself on the edge of my bench. "Etsuko tells me you reside in Fukuoka these days. I visited Fukuoka several times. A fine city, isn't it?"

"Yes, indeed. Fukuoka is my hometown."

"Fukuoka your hometown? But you lived and worked here for years, Ogata-San. Don't we have any claim on you in Nagasaki?"

Ogata-San laughed and leaned his head to one side. "A man might work and make his contribution in one place, but at the end of it all" — he shrugged and smiled wistfully — "at the end of it all, he still wants to go back to the place where he grew up."

Mrs Fujiwara nodded understandingly. Then she said: "I was just remembering, Ogata-San, the days when you were the headmaster at Suichi's school. He used to be so frightened of you."

Ogata-San laughed. "Yes, I remember your Suichi very well. A bright little boy. Very bright."

"Do you really remember him still, Ogata-San?"

"Yes, of course, I remember Suichi. He used to work very hard. A good little boy."

"Yes, he was a good little boy."

Ogata-San pointed at his bowl with his chopsticks. "This is really marvellous," he said.

"Nonsense. I'm sorry I have nothing better to give you."

"No, really, it's delicious."

"Now let me see," said Mrs Fujiwara. "There was a teacher in those days, she was very kind to Suichi. Now what was her name? Suzuki, I think it was, Miss Suzuki. Have you any idea what became of her, Ogata-San?"

"Miss Suzuki? Ah, yes, I recall her quite well. But I'm afraid I've no idea where she could be now."

"She was very kind to Suichi. And there was that other teacher, Kuroda was his name. An excellent young man."

"Kuroda . . ." Ogata-San nodded slowly. "Ah yes, Kuroda. I remember him. A splendid teacher."

"Yes, a most impressive young man. My husband was very struck by him. Do you know what became of him?"

"Kuroda . . ." Ogata-San was still nodding to himself. A streak of sunlight had fallen across his face, lighting up the many wrinkles around his eyes. "Kuroda, now let me see. I ran into him once, quite by accident. That was at the start of the war. I suppose he went off to fight. I've never heard of

150

him since. Yes, an excellent teacher. There are so many from those days I never hear of now."

Someone called out to Mrs Fujiwara and we watched her go hurriedly across the forecourt to her customer's table. She stood there bowing for several moments, then cleared some dishes from the table and disappeared into the kitchen.

Ogata-San watched her, then shook his head. "A great pity to see her like this," he said, in a low voice. I said nothing and continued to eat. Then Ogata-San leaned across the table and asked: "Etsuko, what did you say was the name of her son? The one who's still alive, I mean."

"Kazuo," I whispered.

He nodded, then returned to his bowl of noodles.

Mrs Fujiwara came back a few moments later. "Such a shame I don't have something better to offer you," she said.

"Nonsense," said Ogata-San. "This is delicious. And how is Kazuo-San these days?"

"He's fine. He's in good health, and he enjoys his work."

"Splendid. Etsuko was telling me he works for a motor car company."

"Yes, he's doing very well there. What's more, he's thinking of marrying again."

"Really?"

"He said once he'd never marry again, but he's starting to look ahead to things now. He has no one in mind as of yet, but at least he's started to think ahead."

"That sounds like good sense," Ogata-San said. "Why, he's still quite a young man, isn't he?"

"Of course he is. He still has all his life ahead of him."

"Of course he has. His whole life ahead of him. You must find him a nice young lady, Mrs Fujiwara."

She laughed. "Don't think I haven't tried. But young women are so different these days. It amazes me, how things have changed so much so quickly."

"Indeed, how right you are. Young women these days

are all so headstrong. And forever talking about washing-machines and American dresses. Etsuko here's no different."

"Nonsense, Father."

Mrs Fujiwara laughed again, then said: "I remember the first time I heard of a washing-machine, I couldn't believe anyone would want such a thing. Spending all that money, when you had two good hands to work with. But I'm sure Etsuko wouldn't agree with me."

I was about to say something, but Ogata-San spoke first: "Let me tell you," he said, "what I heard the other day. A man was telling me this, a colleague of Jiro's, in fact. Apparently at the last elections, his wife wouldn't agree with him about which party to vote for. He had to beat her, but she still didn't give way. So in the end, they voted for separate parties. Can you imagine such a thing happening in the old days? Extraordinary."

Mrs Fujiwara shook her head. "Things are so different now," she said, and sighed. "But I hear from Etsuko, Jiro-San is getting on splendidly now. You must be proud of him, Ogata-San."

"Yes, I suppose that boy's getting on well enough. In fact, today he'll be representing his firm at a most important meeting. It appears they're thinking of promoting him again."

"How marvellous."

"It was only last year he was promoted. I suppose his superiors must have a high opinion of him."

"How marvellous. You must be very proud of him."

"He's a determined worker, that one. He always was from an early age. I remember when he was a boy, and all the other fathers were busy telling their children to study harder, I was obliged to keep telling him to play more, it wasn't good for him to work so hard."

Mrs Fujiwara laughed and shook her head. "Yes, Kazuo's a hard worker too," she said. "He's often reading through

152

his paperwork right into the night. I tell him he shouldn't work so hard, but he won't listen."

"No, they never listen. And I must admit, I was much the same. But when you believe in what you're doing, you don't feel like idling away the hours. My wife was always telling me to take it easy, but I never listened."

"Yes, that's just the way Kazuo is. But he'll have to change his ways if he marries again."

"Don't depend on it," Ogata-San said, with a laugh. Then he put his chopsticks neatly together across his bowl. "Why, that was a splendid meal."

"Nonsense. I'm sorry I couldn't offer you something better. Would you care for some more?"

"If you have more to spare me, I'd be delighted. These days, I have to make the best of such good cooking, you know."

"Nonsense," said Mrs Fujiwara again, getting to her feet.

We had not been back long when Jiro came in from work, an hour or so earlier than usual. He greeted his father cheerfully — his show of temper the previous night apparently quite forgotten — before disappearing to take his bath. He returned a little later, dressed in a kimono, humming a song to himself. He seated himself on a cushion and began to towel his hair.

"Well, how did it go?" Ogata-San asked.

"What's that? Oh, the meeting, you mean. It wasn't so bad. Not so bad at all."

I had been on the point of going into the kitchen, but paused at the doorway, waiting to hear what else Jiro had to say. His father, too, continued to look at him. For several moments, Jiro went on towelling his hair, looking at neither of us.

"In fact," he said at last, "I suppose I did rather well. I persuaded their representatives to sign an agreement. Not exactly a contract, but to all purposes the same thing. My boss was quite surprised. It's unusual for them to commit themselves like that. He told me to take the rest of the day off."

"Why, that's splendid news," Ogata-San said, then gave a laugh. He glanced towards me, then back at his son. "That's splendid news."

"Congratulations," I said, smiling at my husband. "I'm so glad."

Jiro looked up, as if noticing me for the first time.

"Why are you standing there like that?" he asked. "I wouldn't mind some tea, you know." He put down his towel and began combing his hair.

That evening, in order to celebrate Jiro's success, I prepared a more elaborate meal than usual. Neither during supper, nor during the rest of the evening, did Ogata-San mention anything of his encounter with Shigeo Matsuda that day. However, just as we began to eat, he said quite suddenly:

"Well, Jiro, I'll be leaving you tomorrow."

Jiro looked up. "You're leaving? Oh, a pity. Well, I hope you enjoyed your visit."

"Yes, I've had a good rest. In fact, I've been with you rather longer than I planned."

"You're welcome, Father," said Jiro. "No need to rush, I assure you."

"Thank you, but I must be getting back now. There's a few things I have to be getting on with."

"Please come and visit us again, whenever it's convenient."

"Father," I said. "You must come and see the baby when it arrives."

Ogata-San smiled. "Perhaps at New Year then," he said. "But I won't bother you much earlier than that, Etsuko. You'll have enough on your hands without having to contend with me."

154

"A pity you caught me at such a busy time," my husband said. "Next time, perhaps, I won't be so hard pressed and we'll have more time to talk."

"Now, don't worry, Jiro. Nothing has pleased me more than to see how much you devote yourself to your work."

"Now this deal's finally gone through," said Jiro, "I'll have a little more time. A shame you have to go back just now. And I was thinking of taking a couple of days off too. Still, it can't be helped, I suppose."

"Father," I said, interrupting, "if Jiro's going to take a few days off, can't you stay another week?"

My husband stopped eating, but did not look up.

"It's tempting," Ogata-San said, "but I really think it's time I went back."

Jiro began to eat once more. "A pity," he said.

"Yes, I really must get the veranda finished before Kikuko and her husband come. They're bound to want to come down in the autumn."

Jiro did not reply, and we all ate in silence for a while. Then Ogata-San said:

"Besides, I can't sit here thinking about chess all day." He laughed, a little strangely.

Jiro nodded, but said nothing. Ogata-San laughed again, then for several moments we continued to eat in silence.

"Do you drink sake these days, Father?" Jiro asked eventually.

"Sake? I take a drop sometimes. Not often."

"Since this is your last evening with us, perhaps we should take some sake."

Ogata-San seemed to consider this for a moment. Finally, he said with a smile: "There's no need to make a fuss about an old man like me. But I'll join you in a cup to celebrate your splendid future."

Jiro nodded to me. I went to the cupboard and brought out a bottle and two cups.

"I always thought you'd go far," Ogata-San was saying.

155

"You always showed promise."

"Just because of what happened today, that's no guarantee they'll give me the promotion," my husband said. "But I suppose my efforts today will have done no harm."

"No, indeed," said Ogata-San. "I doubt if you did yourself much harm today."

They both watched in silence as I poured out the sake. Then Ogata-San laid down his chopsticks and raised his cup.

"Here's to your future, Jiro," he said.

My husband, some food still in his mouth, also raised his cup.

"And to yours, Father," he said.

Memory, I realize, can be an unreliable thing; often it is heavily coloured by the circumstances in which one remembers, and no doubt this applies to certain of the recollections I have gathered here. For instance, I find it tempting to persuade myself it was a premonition I experienced that afternoon, that the unpleasant image which entered my thoughts that day was something altogether different — something much more intense and vivid — than the numerous day-dreams which drift through one's imagination during such long and empty hours.

In all possibility, it was nothing so remarkable. The tragedy of the little girl found hanging from a tree — much more so than the earlier child murders — had made a shocked impression on the neighbourhood, and I could not have been alone that summer in being disturbed by such images.

It was the latter part of the afternoon, a day or two after our outing to Inasa, and I was occupying myself with some small chores around the apartment when I happened to glance out of the window. The wasteground outside must have hardened significantly since the first occasion I had watched that large American car, for now I saw it coming across the uneven surface without undue difficulty. It continued to come nearer, then bumped up on to the concrete beneath my window. The glare on the windscreen prevented me from seeing clearly, but I received a distinct impression the driver was not alone. The car moved around the apartment block and out of my vision.

It must have been just then that it happened, just as I was gazing towards the cottage in a somewhat confused state of mind. With no apparent provocation, that chilling image intruded into my thoughts, and I came away from the window with a troubled feeling. I returned to my housework, trying to put the picture out of my mind, but it was some minutes before I felt sufficiently rid of it to give consideration to the reappearance of the large white car.

It was an hour or so later I saw the figure walking across the wasteground towards the cottage. I shaded my eyes to see more clearly; it was a woman — a thin figure — and she walked with a slow deliberate step. The figure paused outside the cottage for some time, then disappeared behind the sloping roof. I continued to watch, but she did not re-emerge; to all appearances, the woman had gone inside.

For several moments, I remained at the window, unsure what to do. Then finally, I put on some sandals and left the apartment. Outside, the day was at its hottest, and the journey across those few dried acres seemed to take an eternity. Indeed, the walk to the cottage tired me so much that when I arrived I had almost forgotten my original purpose. It was with a kind of shock, then, that I heard voices from within the cottage. One of the voices was Mariko's; the other I did not recognize. I stepped closer to the entrance, but could make out no words. For several moments I remained there, not sure what I should do. Then I slid open the entrance and called out. The voices stopped. I waited another moment, then stepped inside.

Chapter Ten

After the brightness of the day outside, the interior of the cottage seemed cool and dark. Here and there, the sun came in sharply through narrow gaps, lighting up small patches on the tatami. The odour of damp wood seemed as strong as ever.

It took a second or two for my eyes to adjust. There was an old woman sitting on the tatami, Mariko in front of her. In turning to face me, the old woman moved her head with caution as if in fear of hurting her neck. Her face was thin, and had a chalky paleness about it which at first quite unnerved me. She looked to be around seventy or so, though the frailness of her neck and shoulders could have derived from ill-health as much as from age. Her kimono was of a dark sombre colour, the kind normally worn in mourning. Her eyes were slightly hooded and watched me with no apparent emotion.

"How do you do," she said, eventually.

I bowed slightly and returned some greeting. For a second or two, we looked at each other awkwardly.

"Are you a neighbour?" the old woman asked. She had a slow way of speaking her words.

"Yes," I said. "A friend."

She continued to look at me for a moment, then asked: "Have you any idea where the occupant has gone? She's left the child here on her own."

The little girl had shifted her position so that she was sitting alongside the stranger. At the old woman's question, Mariko looked at me intently.

"No, I've no idea," I said.

158

"It's odd," said the woman. "The child doesn't seem to know either. I wonder where she could be. I cannot stay long."

We gazed at each other for a few moments more.

"Have you come far?" I asked.

"Quite far. Please excuse my clothes. I've just been attending a funeral."

"I see." I bowed again.

"A sorrowful occasion," the old woman said, nodding slowly to herself. "A former colleague of my father. My father is too ill to leave the house. He sent me to pay his respects. It was a sorrowful occasion." She passed her gaze around the inside of the cottage, moving her head with the same carefulness. "You have no idea where she is?" she asked again.

"No, I'm afraid not."

"I cannot wait long. My father will be getting anxious."

"Is there perhaps some message I could pass on?" I asked.

The old woman did not answer for a while. Then she said: "You could perhaps tell her I came here and was asking after her. I am a relative. My name is Yasuko Kawada."

"Yasuko-San?" I did my best to conceal my surprise. "You're Yasuko-San, Sachiko's cousin?"

The old woman bowed, and as she did so her shoulders trembled slightly. "If you would tell her I was here and that I was asking after her. You have no idea where she could be?"

Again, I denied any knowledge. The woman began nodding to herself once more.

"Nagasaki is very different now," she said. "This afternoon, I could hardly recognize it."

"Yes," I said. "I suppose it's greatly changed. But do you not live in Nagasaki?"

"We've lived in Nagasaki now for many years. It's greatly

159

changed, as you say. New buildings have appeared, even new streets. It must have been in the spring, the last time I came out into the town. And even since then, new buildings have appeared. I'm certain they were not there in the spring. In fact, on that occasion too, I believe I was attending a funeral. Yes, it was Yamashita-San's funeral. A funeral in the spring seems all the sadder somehow. You are a neighbour, you say? Then I'm very pleased to make your acquaintance." Her face trembled and I saw she was smiling; her eyes had become very thin, and her mouth was curving downwards instead of up. I felt uncomfortable standing in the entryway, but did not feel free to step up to the tatami.

"I'm very pleased to meet you," I said. "Sachiko often mentions you."

"She mentions me?" The woman seemed to consider this for a moment. "We were expecting her to come and live with us. With my father and myself. Perhaps she told you as much."

"Yes, she did."

"We were expecting her three weeks ago. But she has not yet come."

"Three weeks ago? Well, I suppose there must have been some misunderstanding. I know she's preparing to move any day."

The old woman's eyes passed around the cottage once more. "A pity she isn't here," she said. "But if you are her neighbour, then I'm very glad to have made your acquaintance." She bowed to me again, then went on gazing at me. "Perhaps you will pass a message to her," she said.

"Why, certainly."

The woman remained silent for some time. Finally, she said: "We had a slight disagreement, she and I. Perhaps she even told you about it. Nothing more than a misunderstanding, that was all. I was very surprised to find she had packed and left the next day. I was very surprised indeed. I

160

didn't mean to offend her. My father says I am to blame."
She paused for a moment. "I didn't mean to offend her,"
she repeated.

It had never occurred to me before that Sachiko's uncle
and cousin would know nothing of the existence of her
American friend. I bowed again, at a loss for a suitable
reply.

"I've missed her since she left, I confess it," the old
woman continued. "I've missed Mariko-San also. I enjoyed
their company and it was foolish of me to have lost my
temper and said the things I did." She paused again,
turned her face towards Mariko, then back to me. "My
father, in his own way, misses them also. He can hear, you
see. He can hear how much quieter the house is. The other
morning I found him awake and he said it reminded him of
a tomb. Just like a tomb, he said. It would do my father
much good to have them back again. Perhaps she will come
back for his sake."

"I'll certainly convey your feelings to Sachiko-San," I
said.

"For her own sake too," the old woman said. "After all, it
isn't good that a woman should be without a man to guide
her. Only harm can come of such a situation. My father is
ill, but his life is in no danger. She should come back now,
for her own wellbeing if for nothing else." The old woman
began to untie a kerchief lying at her side. "In fact, I
brought these with me," she said. "Just some cardigans I
knitted, nothing more. But it's fine wool. I'd intended to
offer them when she came back, but I brought them with
me today. I first knitted one for Mariko, then I thought I
may as well knit another for her mother." She held up a
cardigan, then looked towards the little girl. Her mouth
curved downwards again as she smiled.

"They look splendid," I said. "It must have taken you a
long time."

"It's fine wool," the woman said again. She wrapped the

kerchief back around the cardigans, then tied it carefully. "Now I must return. My father will be anxious."

She got to her feet and came down off the tatami. I assisted her in putting on her wooden sandals. Mariko had come to the edge of the tatami and the old woman lightly touched the top of the child's head.

"Remember then, Mariko-San," she said, "tell your mother what I told you. And you're not to worry about your kittens. There's plenty of room in the house for them all."

"We'll come soon," Mariko said. "I'll tell Mother."

The woman smiled again. Then she turned to me and bowed. "I'm glad to have made your acquaintance. I cannot stay any longer. My father, you see, is unwell."

"Oh, it's you, Etsuko," Sachiko said, when I returned to her cottage that evening. Then she laughed and said: "Don't look so surprised. You didn't expect me to stay here for ever, did you?"

Articles of clothing, blankets, numerous other items lay scattered over the tatami. I made some appropriate reply and sat down where I would not be in the way. On the floor beside me, I noticed two splendid-looking kimonos I had never seen Sachiko wear. I saw also — in the middle of the floor, packed into a cardboard box — her delicate teaset of pale white china.

Sachiko had opened wide the central partitions to allow the last of the daylight to come into the cottage; despite that, a dimness was fast setting in, and the sunset coming across the veranda barely reached the far corner where Mariko sat watching her mother quietly. Near her, two of the kittens were fighting playfully; the little girl was holding a third kitten in her arms.

"I expect Mariko told you," I said to Sachiko. "There was a visitor for you earlier. Your cousin was here."

"Yes. Mariko told me." Sachiko continued to pack her trunk.

162

"You're leaving in the morning?"

"Yes," she said, with a touch of impatience. Then she gave a sigh and looked up at me. "Yes, Etsuko, we're leaving in the morning." She folded something away into a corner of her trunk.

"You have so much luggage," I said, eventually. "How will you ever carry it all?"

For a little while, Sachiko did not answer. Then, continuing to pack, she said: "You know perfectly well, Etsuko. We'll put it in the car."

I remained silent. She took a deep breath, and glanced across the room to where I was sitting.

"Yes, we're leaving Nagasaki, Etsuko. I assure you, I had every intention of coming to say goodbye once all the packing was finished. I wouldn't have left without thanking you, you've been most kind. Incidentally, as regards the loan, it will be returned to you through the post. Please don't worry about that." She began to pack again.

"Where is it you're going?" I asked.

"Kobe. Everything's decided now, once and for all."

"Kobe?"

"Yes, Etsuko, Kobe. Then after that, America. Frank has arranged everything. Aren't you pleased for me?" She smiled quickly, then turned away again.

I went on watching her. Mariko, too, was watching her. The kitten in her arms was struggling to join its companions on the tatami, but the little girl continued to hold it firmly. Beside her, in the corner of the room, I saw the vegetable box she had won at the *kujibiki* stall; Mariko, it appeared, had converted the box into a house for her kittens.

"Incidentally, Etsuko, that pile over there" — Sachiko pointed — "those items I'll just have to leave behind. I had no idea there was so much. Some of it is of decent enough quality. Please make use of it if you wish. I don't mean any offence, of course. It's merely that some of it is of good quality."

163

"But what about your uncle?" I said. "And your cousin?"

"My uncle?" She gave a shrug. "It was kind of him to have invited me into his household. But I'm afraid I've made other plans now. You have no idea, Etsuko, how relieved I'll be to leave this place. I trust I've seen the last of such squalor." Then she looked across to me once more and laughed. "I can see exactly what you're thinking. I can assure you, Etsuko, you're quite wrong. He won't let me down this time. He'll be here with the car, first thing tomorrow morning. Aren't you pleased for me?" Sachiko looked around at the luggage strewn over the floor and sighed. Then stepping over a pile of clothes, she knelt beside the box containing the teaset, and began filling it with rolls of wool.

"Have you decided yet?" Mariko said, suddenly.

"We can't talk about it now, Mariko," said her mother. "I'm busy now."

"But you said I could keep them. Don't you remember?"

Sachiko shook the cardboard box gently; the china still rattled. She looked around, found a piece of cloth and began tearing it into strips.

"You said I could keep them," Mariko said again.

"Mariko, please consider the situation for a moment. How can we possibly take all those creatures with us?"

"But you said I could keep them."

Sachiko sighed, and for a moment seemed to be considering something. She looked down at the teaset, the pieces of cloth held in her hands.

"You did, Mother," Mariko said. "Don't you remember? You said I could."

Sachiko looked up at her daughter, then over towards the kittens. "Things are different now," she said, tiredly. Then a wave of irritation crossed her face, and she flung down the pieces of cloth. "Mariko, how can you think so much of these creatures? How can we possibly take them with us? No, we'll just have to leave them here."

164

"But you said I could keep them."

Sachiko glared at her daughter for a moment. "Can't you think of anything else?" she said, lowering her voice almost to a whisper. "Aren't you old enough yet to see there are other things besides these filthy little animals? You'll just have to grow up a little. You simply can't have these sentimental attachments for ever. These are just . . . just *animals* don't you see? Don't you understand that, child? Don't you understand?"

Mariko stared back at her mother.

"If you like, Mariko-San," I put in, "I could come and feed them from time to time. Then eventually they'll find homes for themselves. There's no need to worry."

The little girl turned to me. "Mother said I could keep the kittens," she said.

"Stop being so childish," said Sachiko, sharply. "You're being deliberately awkward, as you always are. What does it matter about the dirty little creatures?" She rose to her feet and went over to Mariko's corner. The kittens on the tatami scurried back; Sachiko looked down at them, then took a deep breath. Quite calmly, she turned the vegetable box on to its side — so that the wire-grid panels were facing upwards — reached down and dropped the kittens one by one into the box. She then turned to her daughter; Mariko was still clutching the remaining kitten.

"Give me that," said Sachiko.

Mariko continued to hold the kitten. Sachiko stepped forward and put out her hand. The little girl turned and looked at me.

"This is Atsu," she said. "Do you want to see him, Etsuko-San? This is Atsu."

"Give me that creature, Mariko," Sachiko said. "Don't you understand, it's just an animal. Why can't you understand that, Mariko? Are you really too young? It's not your little baby, it's just an animal, just like a rat or a snake. Now give it to me."

165

Mariko stared up at her mother. Then slowly, she lowered the kitten and let it drop to the tatami in front of her. The kitten struggled as Sachiko lifted it off the ground. She dropped it into the vegetable box and slid shut the wire grid.

"Stay here," she said to her daughter, and picked the box up in her arms. Then as she came past, she said to me: "It's so stupid, these are just animals, what does it matter?"

Mariko rose to her feet and seemed about to follow her mother. Sachiko turned at the entryway and said: "Do as you're told. Stay here."

For a few moments, Mariko remained standing at the edge of the tatami, looking at the doorway where her mother had disappeared.

"Wait for your mother here, Mariko-San," I said to her.

The little girl turned and looked at me. Then the next moment, she had gone.

For a minute or two, I did not move. Then eventually I got to my feet and put on my sandals. From the doorway, I could see Sachiko down by the water, the vegetable box beside her feet; she appeared not to have noticed her daughter standing several yards behind her, just at the point where the ground began to slope down steeply. I left the cottage and made my way to where Mariko was standing.

"Let's go back to the house, Mariko-San," I said, gently.

The little girl's eyes remained on her mother, her face devoid of any expression. Down in front of us, Sachiko knelt cautiously on the bank, then moved the box a little nearer.

"Let's go inside, Mariko," I said again, but the little girl continued to ignore me. I left her and walked down the muddy slope to where Sachiko was kneeling. The sunset was coming through the trees on the opposite bank, and the reeds that grew along the water's edge cast long shadows on the muddy ground around us. Sachiko had found some grass to kneel on, but that too was thick with mud.

"Can't we let them loose?" I said, quietly. "You never know. Someone may want them."

Sachiko was gazing down into the vegetable box through the wire gauze. She slid open a panel, brought out a kitten and shut the box again. She held the kitten in both hands, looked at it for a few seconds, then glanced up at me. "It's just an animal, Etsuko," she said. "That's all it is."

She put the kitten into the water and held it there. She remained like that for some moments, staring into the water, both hands beneath the surface. She was wearing a casual summer kimono, and the corners of each sleeve touched the water.

Then for the first time, without taking her hands from the water, Sachiko threw a glance over her shoulder towards her daughter. Instinctively, I followed her glance, and for one brief moment the two of us were both staring back up at Mariko. The little girl was standing at the top of the slope, watching with the same blank expression. On seeing her mother's face turn to her, she moved her head very slightly; then she remained quite still, her hands behind her back.

Sachiko brought her hands out of the water and stared at the kitten she was still holding. She brought it closer to her face and the water ran down her wrists and arms.

"It's still alive," she said, tiredly. Then she turned to me and said: "Look at this water, Etsuko. It's so dirty." With an air of disgust, she dropped the soaked kitten back into the box and shut it. "How these things struggle," she muttered, and held up her wrists to show me the scratch-marks. Somehow, Sachiko's hair had also become wet; one drop, then another fell from a thin strand which hung down one side of her face.

Sachiko adjusted her position then pushed the vegetable box over the edge of the bank; the box rolled and landed in the water. To prevent it floating, Sachiko leaned forward and held it down. The water came almost halfway up the wire-grid. She continued to hold down the box, then finally pushed it with both hands. The box floated a little way into the river, bobbed and sank further. Sachiko got to her feet, and we both of us watched the box. It continued to float, then caught in the current and began moving more swiftly downstream.

Some movement caught my eye and made me turn. Mariko had run several yards down the river's edge, to a spot where the bank jutted out into the water. She stood there watching the box float on, her face still expressionless. The box caught in some reeds, freed itself and continued its journey. Mariko began to run again. She ran on some distance along the bank, then stopped again to watch the box. By this time, only a small corner was visible above the surface.

"This water's so dirty," Sachiko said. She had been shaking the water off her hands. She squeezed in turn the sleeve-ends of her kimono, then brushed the mud from her knees. "Let's go back inside, Etsuko. The insects here are becoming intolerable."

"Shouldn't we go and get Mariko? It will be dark soon."

Sachiko turned and called her daughter's name. Mariko was now fifty yards or so away, still looking at the water. She did not seem to hear and Sachiko gave a shrug. "She'll come back in time," she said. "Now, I must finish packing before the light goes completely." She began to walk up the slope towards the cottage.

Sachiko lit the lantern and hung it from a low wooden beam. "Don't worry yourself, Etsuko," she said. "She'll be back soon enough." She made her way through the various items strewn over the tatami, and seated herself, as before, in front of the open partitions. Behind her, the sky had

168

become pale and faded.

She began packing again. I sat down at the opposite side of the room and watched her.

"What are your plans now?" I asked. "What will you do once you arrive in Kobe?"

"Everything's been arranged, Etsuko," she said, without looking up. "There's no need to worry. Frank has seen to everything."

"But why Kobe?"

"He has friends there. At the American base. He's been entrusted with a job on a cargo ship, and he'll be in America in a very short time. Then he'll send us the necessary amount of money, and we'll go and join him. He's seen to all the arrangements."

"You mean, he's leaving Japan without you?"

Sachiko laughed. "One needs to be patient, Etsuko. Once he arrives in America, he'll be able to work and send money. It's by far the most sensible solution. After all, it would be so much easier for him to find work once he's back in America. I don't mind waiting a little."

"I see."

"He's seen to everything, Etsuko. He's found a place for us to stay in Kobe, and he's seen to it that we'll get on a ship at almost half the usual cost." She gave a sigh. "You have no idea how pleased I am to be leaving this place."

Sachiko continued to pack. The pale light from outside fell on one side of her face, but her hands and sleeves were caught in the glow from the lantern. It was a strange effect.

"Do you expect to wait long in Kobe?" I asked.

She shrugged. "I'm prepared to be patient, Etsuko. One needs to be patient."

I could not see in the dimness what it was she was folding; it seemed to be giving her some difficulty, for she opened and refolded it several times.

"In any case, Etsuko," she went on, "why would he have gone to all this trouble if he wasn't absolutely sincere? Why

169

would he have gone to all this trouble on my behalf? Sometimes, Etsuko, you seem so doubting. You should be happy for me. Things are working out at last."

"Yes, of course. I'm very happy for you."

"But really, Etsuko, it would be unfair to start doubting him after he's gone to all this trouble. It would be quite unfair."

"Yes."

"And Mariko would be happier there. America is a far better place for a young girl to grow up. Out there, she could do all kinds of things with her life. She could become a business girl. Or she could study painting at college and become an artist. All these things are much easier in America, Etsuko. Japan is no place for a girl. What can she look forward to here?"

I made no reply. Sachiko glanced up at me and gave a small laugh.

"Try and smile, Etsuko," she said. "Things will turn out well in the end."

"Yes, I'm sure they will."

"Of course they will."

"Yes."

For another minute or so, Sachiko continued with her packing. Then her hands became still, and she gazed across the room towards me, her face caught in that strange mixture of light.

"I suppose you think I'm a fool," she said, quietly. "Don't you, Etsuko?"

I looked back at her, a little surprised.

"I realize we may never see America," she said. "And even if we did, I know how difficult things will be. Did you think I never knew that?"

I gave no reply, and we went on staring at each other.

"But what of it?" said Sachiko. "What difference does it make? Why shouldn't I go to Kobe? After all, Etsuko, what do I have to lose? There's nothing for me at my uncle's house. Just a few empty rooms, that's all. I could sit there in a room and grow old. Other than that there'll be nothing. Just empty rooms, that's all. You know that yourself, Etsuko."

"But Mariko," I said. "What about Mariko?"

"Mariko? She'll manage well enough. She'll just have to." Sachiko continued to gaze at me through the dimness, one side of her face in shadow. Then she said: "Do you think I imagine for one moment that I'm a good mother to her?"

I remained silent. Then suddenly, Sachiko laughed.

"Why are we talking like this?" she said, and her hands began to move busily once more. "Everything will turn out well, I assure you. I'll write to you when I reach America. Perhaps, Etsuko, you'll even come and visit us one day. You could bring your child with you."

"Yes, indeed."

"Perhaps you'll have several children by then."

"Yes," I said, laughing awkwardly. "You never know."

Sachiko gave a sigh and lifted both hands into the air. "There's so much to pack," she murmured. "I'll just have to leave some of it behind."

I sat there for some moments, watching her.

"If you wish," I said, eventually, "I could go and look for Mariko. It's getting rather late."

"You'll only tire yourself, Etsuko. I'll finish packing and if she still hasn't come back we could go and look for her together."

"It's all right. I'll see if I can find her. It's nearly dark now."

Sachiko glanced up, then shrugged. "Perhaps you'd best take the lantern with you," she said. "It's quite slippery along the bank."

I rose to my feet and took the lantern down from the beam. The shadows moved across the cottage as I walked with it towards the doorway. As I was leaving, I glanced back towards Sachiko. I could see only her silhouette, seated before the open partitions, the sky behind her turned almost to night.

Insects followed my lantern as I made my way along the river. Occasionally, some creature would become trapped inside, and I would then have to stop and hold the lantern still until it had found its way out.

In time, the small wooden bridge appeared on the bank ahead of me. While crossing it, I stopped for a moment to gaze at the evening sky. As I recall, a strange sense of tranquillity came over me there on that bridge. I stood there for some minutes, leaning over the rail, listening to the sounds of the river below me. When finally I turned, I saw my own shadow, cast by the lantern, thrown across the wooden slats of the bridge.

"What are you doing here?" I asked, for the little girl was before me, sat crouched beneath the opposite rail. I came forward until I could see her more clearly under my lantern. She was looking at her palms and said nothing.

"What's the matter with you?" I said. "Why are you sitting here like this?"

The insects were clustering around the lantern. I put it down in front of me, and the child's face became more sharply illuminated. After a long silence, she said: "I don't want to go away. I don't want to go away tomorrow."

I gave a sigh. "But you'll like it. Everyone's a little frightened of new things. You'll like it over there."

"I don't want to go away. And I don't like him. He's like a pig."

"You're not to speak like that," I said, angrily. We stared at each other for a moment, then she looked back down at her hands.

"You mustn't speak like that," I said, more calmly. "He's very fond of you, and he'll be just like a new father. Everything will turn out well, I promise."

The child said nothing. I sighed again.

"In any case," I went on, "if you don't like it over there, we can always come back."

This time she looked up at me questioningly.

"Yes, I promise," I said. "If you don't like it over there, we'll come straight back. But we have to try it and see if we like it there. I'm sure we will."

The little girl was watching me closely. "Why are you holding that?" she asked.

"This? It just caught around my sandal, that's all."

"Why are you holding it?"

"I told you. It caught around my foot. What's wrong with you?" I gave a short laugh. "Why are you looking at me like that? I'm not going to hurt you."

Without taking her eyes from me, she rose slowly to her feet.

"What's wrong with you?" I repeated.

The child began to run, her footsteps drumming along the wooden boards. She stopped at the end of the bridge and stood watching me suspiciously. I smiled at her and picked up the lantern. The child began once more to run.

A half-moon had appeared above the water and for several quiet moments I remained on the bridge, gazing at it. Once, through the dimness, I thought I could see Mariko running along the riverbank in the direction of the cottage.

Chapter Eleven

At first, I was sure someone had walked past my bed and out of my room, closing the door quietly. Then I became more awake, and I realized how fanciful an idea this was.

I lay in bed listening for further noises. Quite obviously, I had heard Niki in the next room; she had complained throughout her stay of being unable to sleep well. Or possibly there had been no noises at all, I had awoken again during the early hours from habit.

The sound of birds came from outside, but my room was still in darkness. After several minutes I rose and found my dressing gown. When I opened my door, the light outside was very pale. I stepped further on to the landing and almost by instinct cast a glance down to the far end of the corridor, towards Keiko's door.

Then, for a moment, I was sure I had heard a sound come from within Keiko's room, a small clear sound amidst the singing of the birds outside. I stood still, listening, then began to walk towards the door. There came more noises, and I realized they were coming from the kitchen downstairs. I remained on the landing for a moment, then made my way down the staircase.

Niki was coming out of the kitchen and started on seeing me.

"Oh, Mother, you gave me a real fright."

In the murky light of the hallway, I could see her thin figure in a pale dressing gown holding a cup in both her hands.

"I'm sorry, Niki. I thought perhaps you were a burglar."

My daughter took a deep breath, but still seemed shaken.

Then she said: "I couldn't sleep very well. So I thought I might as well make some coffee."

"What time is it now?"

"About five, I suppose."

She went into the living room, leaving me standing at the foot of the stairs. I went to the kitchen to make myself coffee before going to join her. In the living room, Niki had opened the curtains and was sitting astride a hard-backed chair, looking emptily out into the garden. The grey light from the window fell on her face.

"Will it rain again, do you think?" I asked.

She shrugged and continued to look out of the window. I sat down near the fireplace and watched her. Then she sighed tiredly and said:

"I don't seem to sleep very well. I keep having these bad dreams all the time."

"That's worrying, Niki. At your age you should have no problems sleeping."

She said nothing and went on looking at the garden.

"What kind of bad dreams do you have?" I asked.

"Oh, just bad dreams."

"Bad dreams about what, Niki?"

"Just bad dreams," she said, suddenly irritated. "What does it matter what they're about?"

We fell silent for a moment. Then Niki said without turning:

"I suppose Dad should have looked after her a bit more, shouldn't he? He ignored her most of the time. It wasn't fair really."

I waited to see if she would say more. Then I said: "Well, it's understandable enough. He wasn't her real father, after all."

"But it wasn't fair really."

Outside, I could see, it was nearly daylight. A lone bird was making its noises somewhere close by the window.

"Your father was rather idealistic at times," I said. "In

175

those days, you see, he really believed we could give her a happy life over here."

Niki shrugged. I watched her for a little longer, then said: "But you see, Niki, I knew all along. I knew all along she wouldn't be happy over here. But I decided to bring her just the same."

My daughter seemed to consider this for a moment. "Don't be silly," she said, turning to me, "how could you have known? And you did everything you could for her. You're the last person anyone could blame."

I remained silent. Her face, devoid of any make-up, looked very young.

"Anyway," she said, "sometimes you've got to take risks. You did exactly the right thing. You can't just watch your life wasting away."

I put down the coffee cup I had been holding and stared past her, out into the garden. There were no signs of rain and the sky seemed clearer than on previous mornings.

"It would have been so stupid," Niki went on, "if you'd just accepted everything the way it was and just stayed where you were. At least you made an effort."

"As you say. Now let's not discuss it any further."

"It's so stupid the way people just waste away their lives."

"Let's not discuss it any further," I said, more firmly. "There's no point in going over all that now."

My daughter turned away again. We sat without talking for a little while, then I rose to my feet and came closer to the window.

"It looks a much better morning today," I said. "Perhaps the sun will come out. If it does, Niki, we could go for a walk. It would do us a lot of good."

"I suppose so," she mumbled.

When I left the living room, my daughter was still sitting astride her chair, her chin supported by a hand, gazing emptily out into the garden.

176

When the telephone rang, Niki and I were finishing breakfast in the kitchen. It had rung for her so frequently during the previous few days that it seemed natural she should be the one to go and answer it. By the time she returned, her coffee had grown cold.

"Your friends again?" I asked.

She nodded, then went over to switch on the kettle.

"Actually, Mother," she said, "I'll have to go back this afternoon. Is that all right?" She was standing with one hand on the handle of the kettle, the other on her hip.

"Of course it's all right. It's been very nice having you here, Niki."

"I'll come and see you again soon. But I've really got to be getting back now."

"You don't have to apologize. It's very important you lead your own life now."

Niki turned away and waited for her kettle. The windows above the sink unit had misted over a little, but outside the sun was shining. Niki poured herself coffee, then sat down at the table.

"Oh, by the way, Mother," she said. "You know that friend I was telling you about, the one writing the poem about you?"

I smiled. "Oh yes. Your friend."

"She wanted me to bring back a photo or something. Of Nagasaki. Have you got anything like that? An old postcard or something?"

"I should think I could find something for you. How absurd" — I gave a laugh — "Whatever can she be writing about me?"

"She's a really good poet. She's been through a lot, you see. That's why I told her about you."

"I'm sure she'll write a marvellous poem, Niki."

"Just an old postcard, anything like that. Just so she can see what everything was like."

177

"Well, Niki, I'm not so sure. It has to show what *every-thing* was like, does it?"

"You know what I mean."

I laughed again. "I'll have a look for you later."

Niki had been buttering a piece of toast, but now she began to scrape some butter off again. My daughter has been thin since childhood, and the idea that she was concerned at becoming fat amused me. I watched her for a moment.

"Still," I said, eventually, "it's a pity you're leaving today. I was about to suggest we went to the cinema this evening."

"The cinema? Why, what's on?"

"I don't know what kind of films they show these days. I was hoping you'd know more about it."

"Actually, Mother, it's ages since we went to a film together, isn't it? Not since I was little." Niki smiled, and for a moment her face became child-like. Then she put down her knife and gazed at her coffee cup. "I don't go to see films much either," she said. "There's always loads on in London, but we don't go much."

"Well, if you prefer, there's always the theatre. The bus takes you right up to the theatre now. I don't know what they have on at the moment, but we could find out. Is that the local paper there, just behind you?"

"Well, Mother, don't bother. There's not much point."

"I think they do quite good plays sometimes. Some quite modern ones. It'll say in the paper."

"There's not much point, Mother. I'll have to go back today anyhow. I'd like to stay, but I've really got to get back."

"Of course, Niki. There's no need to apologize." I smiled at her across the table. "As a matter of fact, it's a great comfort to me you have good friends you enjoy being with. You're always welcome to bring any of them here."

"Yes, Mother, thank you."

The spare bedroom Niki had been using was small and stark; the sun was streaming into it that morning.

"Will this do for your friend?" I asked, from the doorway.

Niki was packing her suitcase on the bed and glanced up briefly at the calendar I had found. "That's fine," she said.

I stepped further into the room. From the window, I could see the orchard below and the neat rows of thin young trees. The calendar I was holding had originally offered a photograph for each month, but all but the last had been torn away. For a moment, I regarded the remaining picture.

"Don't give me anything important," Niki said. "If there isn't anything, it doesn't matter."

I laughed and laid the picture down on the bed alongside her other things. "It's just an old calendar, that's all. I've no idea why I've kept it."

Niki pushed some hair back behind her ear, then continued packing.

"I suppose," I said, eventually, "you plan to go on living in London for the time being."

She gave a shrug. "Well, I'm quite happy there."

"You must send my best wishes to all your friends."

"All right, I will."

"And to David. That was his name, wasn't it?"

She gave another shrug, but said nothing. She had brought with her three separate pairs of boots and now she was struggling to find a way of putting them in her case.

"I suppose, Niki, you don't have any plans yet to be getting married?"

"What do I want to get married for?"

"I was just asking."

"Why should I get married? What's the point of that?"

"You plan to just go on — living in London, do you?"

"Well, why should I get married? That's so stupid,

179

Mother." She rolled up the calendar and packed it away. "So many women just get brainwashed. They think all there is to life is getting married and having a load of kids."

I continued to watch her. Then I said: "But in the end, Niki, there isn't very much else."

"God, Mother, there's plenty of things I could do. I don't want to just get stuck away somewhere with a husband and a load of screaming kids. Why are you going on about it suddenly anyway?" The lid of her suitcase would not shut. She pushed down at it impatiently.

"I was only wondering what your plans were, Niki," I said, with a laugh. "There's no need to get so cross. Of course, you must do what you choose."

She opened the lid again and adjusted some of the contents.

"Now, Niki, there's no need to get so cross."

This time, she managed to close the lid. "God knows why I brought so much," she muttered to herself.

"What do you say to people, Mother?" Niki asked. "What do you say when they ask where I am?"

My daughter had decided she need not leave until after lunch and we had come out walking through the orchard behind the house. The sun was still out, but the air was chilly. I gave her a puzzled look.

"I just tell them you're living in London, Niki. Isn't that the truth?"

"I suppose so. But don't they ask what I'm doing? Like that old Mrs Waters the other day?"

"Yes, sometimes they ask. I tell them you're living with your friends. Really, Niki, I had no idea you were so concerned about what people thought of you."

"I'm not."

We continued to walk slowly. In many places, the ground had become marshy.

180

"I suppose you don't like it very much, do you, Mother?"

"Like what, Niki?"

"The way things are with me. You don't like me living away. With David and all that."

We had come to the end of the orchard. Niki stepped out on to a small winding lane and crossed to the other side, towards the wooden gates of a field. I followed her. The grass field was large and rose gradually as it spread away from us. At its crest, we could see two thin sycamore trees against the sky.

"I'm not ashamed of you, Niki," I said. "You must live as you think best."

My daughter was gazing at the field. "They used to have horses here, didn't they?" she said, putting her arms up on to the gate. I looked, but there were no horses to be seen.

"You know, it's strange," I said. "I remember when I first married, there was a lot of argument because my husband didn't want to live with his father. You see, in those days that was still quite expected in Japan. There was a lot of argument about that."

"I bet you were relieved," Niki said, not taking her eyes from the field.

"Relieved? About what?"

"About not having to live with his father."

"On the contrary, Niki. I would have been happy if he'd lived with us. Besides, he was a widower. It's not a bad thing at all, the old Japanese way."

"Obviously, you'd say that now. I bet that's not what you thought at the time though."

"But Niki, you really don't understand. I was very fond of my father-in-law." I looked at her for a moment, then finally gave a laugh. "Perhaps you're right. Perhaps I was relieved he didn't come to live with us. I don't remember now." I reached forward and touched the top of the wooden gate. A little moisture came away on my fingers. I realized Niki was watching me and I held up my hand to show her.

181

"There's still some frost," I said.

"Do you still think about Japan a lot, Mother?"

"I suppose so." I turned back to the field. "I have a few memories."

Two ponies had appeared near the sycamore trees. For a moment they stood quite still, in the sunshine, side by side.

"That calendar I gave you this morning," I said. "That's a view of the harbour in Nagasaki. This morning I was remembering the time we went there once, on a day-trip. Those hills over the harbour are very beautiful."

The ponies moved slowly behind the trees.

"What was so special about it?" said Niki.

"Special?"

"About the day you spent at the harbour."

"Oh, there was nothing special about it. I was just remembering it, that's all. Keiko was happy that day. We rode on the cable-cars." I gave a laugh and turned to Niki. "No, there was nothing special about it. It's just a happy memory, that's all."

My daughter gave a sigh. "Everything's so quiet out here," she said. "I don't remember things being this quiet."

"Yes, it must seem quiet after London."

"I suppose it gets a bit boring sometimes, out here on your own."

"But I enjoy the quiet, Niki. I always think it's so truly like England out here."

I turned away from the field, and for a moment looked back towards the orchard behind us.

"All those trees weren't here when we first came," I said, eventually. "It was all fields, and you could see the house from here. When your father first brought me down here, Niki, I remember thinking how so truly like England everything looked. All these fields, and the house too. It was just the way I always imagined England would be and I was so pleased."

182

Niki took a deep breath and moved away from the gate. "We'd better be getting back," she said. "I'll have to be going fairly soon."

As we walked back through the orchard, the sky seemed to cloud over.

"I was just thinking the other day," I said, "perhaps I should sell the house now."

"Sell it?"

"Yes. Move somewhere smaller perhaps. It's just an idea."

"You want to sell the house?" My daughter gave me a concerned look. "But it's a really nice house."

"But it's so large now."

"But it's a really nice house, Mother. It'd be a shame."

"I suppose so. It was just an idea, Niki, that's all."

I would like to have seen her to the railway station — it is only a few minutes' walk — but the idea seemed to embarrass her. She left shortly after lunch with an oddly self-conscious air, as if she were leaving without my approval. The afternoon had turned grey and windy, and I stood in the doorway as she walked down to the end of the drive. She was dressed in the same tight-fitting clothes she had arrived in, and her suitcase made her drag her step a little. When she reached the gate, Niki glanced back and seemed surprised to find me still standing at the door. I smiled and waved to her.

THE BURIED GIANT

In post-Arthurian Britain, the wars that once raged between the Saxons and the Britons have finally ceased. Axl and Beatrice, an elderly British couple, set off to visit their son, whom they haven't seen in years. And, because a strange mist has caused mass amnesia throughout the land, they can scarcely remember anything about him. As they are joined on their journey by a Saxon warrior, his orphan charge, and an illustrious knight, Axl and Beatrice slowly begin to remember the dark and troubled past they all share. By turns savage, suspenseful, and intensely moving, *The Buried Giant* is a luminous meditation on the act of forgetting and the power of memory, an extraordinary tale of love, vengeance, and war.

Fiction

NOCTURNES
Five Stories of Music and Nightfall

With the clarity and precision that have become his trademarks, Kazuo Ishiguro interlocks five short pieces of fiction to create a world that resonates with emotion, heartbreak, and humor. Here is a fragile, once-famous singer, turning his back on the one thing he loves; a music junkie with little else to offer his friends but opinion; a songwriter who inadvertently breaks up a marriage; a jazz musician who thinks the answer to his career lies in changing his physical appearance; and a young cellist whose tutor has devised a remarkable way to foster his talent. Music is a central part of their lives and, in one way or another, delivers them to an epiphany.

Fiction

As children, Kathy, Ruth, and Tommy were students at Hailsham, an exclusive boarding school secluded in the English countryside. It was a place of mercurial cliques and mysterious rules, where teachers were constantly reminding their charges of how special they were. Now, years later, Kathy is a young woman. Ruth and Tommy have reentered her life. And for the first time she is beginning to look back at their shared past and understand just what it is that makes them special—and how that gift will shape the rest of their time together.

Fiction

THE UNCONSOLED

The Unconsoled is at once a gripping psychological mystery, a wicked satire of the cult of art, and a poignant character study of a man whose public life has accelerated beyond his control. Ryder, a renowned pianist, has come to a nameless Central European city to give the most important performance of his life. Instead, he finds himself diverted on a series of cryptic and infuriating errands that nevertheless provide him with vital clues to his own past. Ishiguro creates a work that is itself a virtuoso performance, strange, haunting, and resonant with humanity and wit.

Fiction

THE REMAINS OF THE DAY

The Remains of the Day is a profoundly compelling portrait of the perfect English butler and of his fading, insular world in postwar England. At the end of his three decades of service at Darlington Hall, Stevens embarks on a country drive, during which he looks back over his career to reassure himself that he has served humanity by serving "a great gentleman." But lurking in his memory are doubts about the true nature of Lord Darlington's "greatness" and graver doubts about his own faith in the man he served.

Fiction

WHEN WE WERE ORPHANS

Born in early-twentieth-century Shanghai, Banks was orphaned at the age of nine after the separate disappearances of his parents. Now, more than twenty years later, he is a celebrated figure in London society, yet the investigative expertise that has garnered him fame has done little to illuminate the circumstances of his parents' alleged kidnappings. Banks travels to the seething, labyrinthine city of his memory in hopes of solving the mystery of his own, painful past, only to find that war is ravaging Shanghai beyond recognition—and that his own recollections are proving as difficult to trust as the people around him.

Fiction

AN ARTIST OF THE FLOATING WORLD

In the face of the misery in his homeland, the artist Masuji Ono was unwilling to devote his art solely to the celebration of physical beauty. Instead, he put his work in the service of the imperialist movement that led Japan into World War II. Now, as the mature Ono struggles through the aftermath of that war, his memories of his youth and of the "floating world"—the nocturnal world of pleasure, entertainment, and drink—offer him both escape and redemption, even as they punish him for betraying his early promise. Indicted by society for its defeat and reviled for his past aesthetics, he relives the passage through his personal history that makes him both a hero and a coward but, above all, a human being.

Fiction

A WILDERNESS STATION
Selected Stories, 1968–1994
by Alice Munro

Spanning almost thirty years and settings that range from big cities to small towns and farmsteads of rural Canada, this magnificent collection brings together twenty-eight stories by a writer of unparalleled wit, generosity, and emotional power. In *A Wilderness Station: Selected Stories, 1968–1994*, Alice Munro makes lives that seem small unfold until they are revealed to be as spacious as prairies and locates the moments of love and betrayal, desire and forgiveness, that change those lives forever. A traveling salesman during the Depression takes his children with him on an impromptu visit to a former girlfriend. A poor girl steels herself to marry a rich fiancé she can't quite manage to love. An abandoned woman tries to choose between the opposing pleasures of seduction and solitude. To read these stories is to succumb to the spell of a true narrative sorcerer, a writer who enchants her readers utterly even as she restores them to their truest selves.

Fiction

MOTHERING SUNDAY
by Graham Swift

On an unseasonably warm spring day in 1924, Jane Fairchild, a twenty-two-year-old maid at an English country house, meets with her secret lover, the young heir of a neighboring estate. He is about to be married to a woman more befitting his social status, and the time has come to end the affair—but events unfold in ways Jane could never have predicted.

Fiction

ABSOLUTELY ON MUSIC
Conversations
by Haruki Murakami and Seiji Ozawa

In *Absolutely on Music*, internationally acclaimed author Haruki Murakami sits down with his friend Seiji Ozawa, the revered former conductor of the Boston Symphony Orchestra, for a series of conversations on their shared passion: music. Over the course of two years, Murakami and Ozawa discuss everything from Brahms to Beethoven, from Leonard Bernstein to Glenn Gould, from Bartók to Mahler, and from pop-up orchestras to opera. They listen to and dissect recordings of some of their favorite performances, and Murakami questions Ozawa about his career conducting orchestras around the world. Culminating in Murakami's ten-day visit to the banks of Lake Geneva to observe Ozawa's retreat for young musicians, the book is interspersed with ruminations on record collecting, jazz clubs, orchestra halls, film scores, and much more. A deep reflection on the essential nature of both music and writing, *Absolutely on Music* is an unprecedented glimpse into the minds of two maestros.

Fiction

VINTAGE INTERNATIONAL
Available wherever books are sold.
www.vintagebooks.com

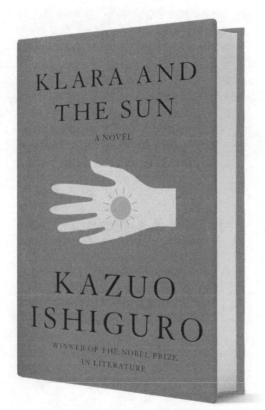